ANGJELINA MARKU

WINTER OF THE CENTURY

- NOVEL -

Prishtina - 2018

Published in the United States of America
By Lulu Press Enterprises, Inc.
South Carolina (USA)
Copyright © 2020 by Angjelina Marku

Library of Congress Cataloging – in – Publication Data
Marku, Angjelina, 1968 –
Winter of the Century, Novel

Editor of Albanian Language Edition: Violeta Allmuça, author, novelist, and linguist
Editor of English Language Edition: Carol Vollmer Pope, MBA
Editor of English Language Edition: Martin Barillas, author, journalist,
and former US Diplomat
Albanian language original title: *"Dimri i Shekullit"*

ISBN: 978-1-71689-767-2
Imprint: Lulu.com

I was, was not, because I was counted as a woman.
If you see yourself with the eyes of an intelligent,
you will never be lost.
Time gives you three types of kisses: a kiss of
longing, happyness and of silence.

In Kärtner Ring 17 is located "Cafe Schwarzenberg", one of the most famous restaurants of Vienna, with a tradition of over a hundred and fifty years, a place were customer service is at the pinnacle of success, providing the best attention to its customers coming from all corners of Austria in order to appreciate and enjoy the typical meals of Vienna, prepared with love in this legendary place.

A young lady, working as a head cook in the restaurant, needed only one minute, including her walk through the traffick lights, to reach the middle of Schwarzenberg Square, righ where the Metro Station (for Car 71) is located, so that Ela could hop in to travel straight towards Kaiserebersdorf.

Chapter 1

Every New Year's Eve is bothersome for all of those working in the field of Gastronomy and Cuisine. The same thing was occuring today in "Cafe Schwarzenberg". Besides a myriad of meals being prepared, in the kitchen were working very hard the Chef and dishwashers. Everyone but Ela, was overwhelmed with work, a junior cook, whose agility gave the impression that she was on top of the game. When the watch was marking 10:30 PM, Ela runned into her locker room, undressed her work uniform and went back in the kitchen, she quickly hugged all her colleagues and wished them a successful new year, then she run away swiftly. This time Ela did not exit from the back door, she walked across the dining room of the restaurant. After greeting all food servers, she escaped from the dining hall filled with guests awaiting huriedly to receive their meals and punctual service.

For less than thirty seconds Ela encountered a street full of snowflakes that were falling relentlessly. Fully relieved from her job, she relaxed her lungs full of fresh air and was waiting infront of the traffick light. That night, the first thing that came to her attention was the grey sky, with the appearance of hundreds and thousands of colors, that were intertwined within seconds, then she enjoyed well decorated houses and bright trees veiled by colorful lights. In those moments, a few musical sounds that were coming from Hotel Imperial, attracted Ela; the hotel was on the other side of the street, afterwards a large number of people whose laughs melted within the fireworks' sounds that covered the sky of Vienna. For a minute Ela was looking at the door attendants in front of the hotel, that were extremely busy and were not looking at the snow falling infinitely; they were not even looking at hotel guests and other pedestrans that were exchanging greetings and kissing each other very openly.

Simply those Door attendants were interested towards the satisfaction of hotel guests and certainly delighted with the tips they were receiving. The only thing bothering them were the taxicab drivers in this intersection. Taxi drivers were creating an unpleasant confusion while driving uncontrollably their vehicles, however the presence of Police was ensuring a constant circulation throughout the corners of Vienna. With all the noise, the lady cook was enjoying something magical. In her fatherland she had never experienced these gorgeous images, perhaps in the past but very rarely and in a different setting. Mesmerized, Ela was lost in front of the traffick light and forgot that she was waiting for the green light longer than a few minutes. From head to toe, from the exciting wave of celebrations, she could not control herself, she was speaking out loud and other pedestrians were listening as she spoke in her native tongue:

-    Oh God! – Why have you forgotten my people?

Those sitting close to her had no idea what she was saying, they saw her wipe her eyes with the mantle of her scarf, those eyes were turbulent from the cold snow, that was dripping below her rosy face. Lost in the exhilerating atmosphere of that night and surrounded by the sweet fierceness of her beloved weather, finally she noticed that red light went away and over the white lanes, covered by snow, were walking hundreds of people. Everyone was in a hurry except for her, because of her cheap boots that were very slippery and unfortunately Ela could not walk as fast as the others.

Moreover, she wanted to enjoy a few moments of happiness with these strange people below the bright lights and large flakes that were falling, covering with white the prettiest city in the world. Ela loved such a weather, even though, she was walking without a hat or umbrella it was not bothersome to her. Indeed, the oposite was true, when the slow flakes were melting on her warm cheeks and covering her black hair, she felt a huge satisfaccion, she was very happy.

As a result, unhurriedly, she headed towards the nearest metro station that was right in the middle of Schwarzenberg Plaza. To get there, she had to cross a second traffic light on the left side. This time she broke the traffic rules. Took a peek on the left and right sides, shook abruptly, and suddenly she found herself in front of the statue of Franz Joseph, the emperor of Austria, who brought to her a deeply rooted fear. She had never realized the fact of it being such a tall statue. Her body was shivering. She thought the person on top of the horse was following her with his eyes and was doing all of this without moving his head neither his bronze hat, that was protecting his face from the white snowflakes. The girl was desperately looking to get away, but she really saw the tip of the prince's tall boots that were poking the horse's back. The horse was even lifting his tail and shaking his right foot in the air and started to slowly hit the base. Ela had little knowledge about the history of this statue, but simply she understood that the inseparable two were getting ready to go somewere. Frightened, she closed her eyes under the snowflakes and breathing deeply she felt that everything went to the right place.

- What is happening with me? Is this hallucination? – she recurred a few times. To be frightened from something that is made by human hands is simply funny, - Ela was thinking, then she entered at the house with glass, were other travelers were waiting. Immediately she turned her back to the statue, she tried to eliminate the fear under the sounds of attractive songs, fireworks and the smell of alcohol that was coming from a crew of youngsters, unlimited smiles and laughs that were exchanged among themselves. But, her desire to enjoy a magical night, went away. Everything that she wanted today was to go as far as possible from this place. Shaking from fear she could not afford the north winds and fearful thoughts, that were biting her head. Untied slightly her wool scarf around her neck because it was taking her breadth away and pulled out her hat, cell phone and headphones. She wanted to listen and see something different from all that was around her. She adjusted well her headphones in her ears and tucked in her cotton made hat on top of her head, reaching almost her nose. She turned on the cell phone screen and viewing one by one the pages of internet while waiting for the metro. When she gathered herself together, felt a soft touch on her shoulders. She made a turn of 180 degrees. In front of her was a lady on her eighties, that lifted her hat over her blue eyes, with her skinny and fragile fingers. While shaken, she saw her blue eyes and thought that she knew her.

- No, no, she is not the lady with red hair, who comes in the kitchen every Thursday and leaves a special tip for the kitchen personnel, as an appreciation to a good food that we serve, - Ela said to herself in silence.

Eventhough she did not know her, Ela responded respectfully to the old lady:

-	You are welcome, please. What can I do for you?

The old lady smiled and asked: - What time is it?

Ela was relieved, she took off her headphones with her naked hands was looking for her watch on her purse filled with many items. Now she remembered of her cell phone she was carrying on the other hand and immediately was looking at the watch. Then she said, 34 minutes had passed the twenty second hour. The old lady was thankful, meanwhile Ela was surprised with the positive attitude of this strange lady. However, the sweetness of the old lady made Ela feel more secure in herself eventhough in the world beyond that glassy bus station 'luxurious hut' was falling a beleaguering snow.

Chapter 2

After a few minutes, the waves of metro cars were felt through the rail, it stopped in front of their feet. Travelers were getting in the metro as if something were following them. Ela was afraid to think of what was pressuring them, except for snow, to get in a hurry inside the metro cars. As she was distracting her mind, the doors of the metro car were closed, and filled with people was headed towards the city's cemetery. At the moment every passenger was trying to get a seat that was comfortable to them, except for a few youngsters that were pleased to stand up while drinking beers and raki. With bottles on their hands, they were swearing at each other without any shame nor guilt. As always Ela wanted to sit down on the right side of metro in a seat that enabled her to appreciate the beauty of the streets of Vienna. Just like always, she sat in her favorite chair, she crossed her feet over the other, layed her elbow at the edge of a side window, while squeezing her chin inside her hand palm, she glanced her perspective beyond the glass, looking at how the snowflakes were covering this gorgeous part of a unique metropolis.

The metro was roaming through the memorial plaza. The multitude of colors that were brightening the white man's statue, dissolved on a marble, everytime she was passing through the edges of the Park. Today the brightness that penetrated through the metro's window, opened widely the eyes of the kitchen's lady cheff. The image of a powerful soldier instilled in her a twofolded sadness. The feeling that the hero was moving was undoubted. The statue was moving with an enormous speed. Ela was looking at how the knight was throwing the flag from his right hand to the left and the armor that he held so tightly on his chest, he grabbed with his right hand, pointing it towards a metro filled with passengers. She bowed her head and was expecting to hear a violent performance of swordsmanship or a barrage of bullets.

Nothing.

Her fear was also seen by the old lady, who was sitting at the left of Ela, while looking at how the young lady was reacting before all these occurrences, and silently she maintained her straight posture, looking up front as if she had seen nothing.

- Is this still a hallucination, - she said to herself.

The word that she had just said, gave her courage to direct her view towards the open window that was dividing the world of the living and dead. It was viewed only by Ela, who continued to think of her hallucinations. Shaken, she was determined to root out the emotions of fear and she was focused completely outside the metro that was cutting through the walls of "Belvedere" Palace. For the third time she begun to deeply breath, due to what she observed. Shadows, white and black were crawling through the walls of the palace, and appeared to be attractive, but mad with one another. They were looking at Ela for a second as if they were advising her, as they were in a hurry to meet with her in a world that did not belong to her. Ela, while frozen,

9

continued to observe the shadows that under the ugly storm were becoming smaller on her eyes, while the metro operator was accelerating faster than before. The metro was leaving monuments, statues, palaces, and thousands of people behind that were celebrating in the Schwarzenberg Plaza. The whole first neighborhood of Vienna remained behind the back of Ela, whose face was pegged on the frozen glass, remaining shocked up until the doors of metro car were opened again and a group of noisy youngsters entered and were beating up the windows of the metro in front of her feeble face just like a ghost. One of the guys that was speaking with his friend outside the metro car, was keeping the door open while pressing the red button of the car and the cold air of a powerful storm entered inside and was hitting straight the yellow face of Ela. On that very same moment, Ela took a deep breadth, just like recently awakening in the Emergency Room. She viewed the passengers around. They had not seen something extraordinary. While she was not fully certain that the experience of those few minutes was entirely a hallucination, she asked one of the young guys, on what was the next station?

She wanted to be assured by someone that she was still in the metro car and that her mind was in a good shape. The young man with a red face caused from the cold weather replied:

- Enkplaz is coming up.
- Aha, thank you, - she responded and pulled out her cell phone.

Amazingly the network was not working. She was entirely electrified. Ela tried to call her parents, but everything was going nowhere. She observed the people. Everyone was happy but her. Confused, she turned her head towards the old lady and encountered her blue eyes following her, just like a camera footage that is following an actor.

The lady with a kashmere fur grinned up to the moment when she captured the words:

- A bad weather in Europe.

- I have read in the paper that this is the winter of the century, - was affirming a man holding
tight on the side bars of the metro car. The old woman widely opened her eyes, appeared surprised. The words "Winter of the Century" in Albanian sounded very abrasive to her. She did not feel good. She held on to her brown purse and was tucked inside the sleeves of her coat, that fitted well in her body. The old lady had heard from her grandmother the terrible story of Winter of the Century. This winter comes once in a hundred years and takes many lives. The old lady rapidly moved her timid eye lids, pulled up her hat that had all quietly come down to her lips and her memory still lucid, brought her to those childhood years, in the first floor, of the fifth district of Vienna, Anitagasse Ave., where she had lived together with her grandma Gertrude, grandpa Kristof, aunty Gabriela and her father Johann, whom she had never met, just like her mom, who she had never met either.

Chapter 3

Melani had never forgotten her past. She remembered vividly her last night with her grandma, who she loved so much. She remembered how the two ladies could not sleep and silence was fighting both grandma and grand daughter, but not the full moon that was playing, satisfying the ladies, in the warm living room. Laid down near each other, with clean blankets as always, it was Melani that broke the dull silence of quiet nights. Even on that special night, she stuck in her head in the cover of wonders, pulled up her thick blanket, and, when she wanted to share with her grandma what she was looking at, the old lady begun her sad story. Then Melani relieved her hands and feet down, exposed her head from the magic cover that she really loved, grabbed her

11

thin hand and focused her eyes at the fire that was turning slowly into ashes inside the fireplace. Gertrude kissed the brown hair of her grand daughter, that was well refined and scented with a rose smell of shampoo and begun to talk about her past in the half lit room:

-      My dear, the winter of 1939 is not easily forgotten and for this reason they named it as the "Winter of the Century". In Vienna winters usually were never so harsh, because the snow was melting for a short period of time. Even in the Christmas Eve of that year, when the first flakes begun to cover the ground, local people were extremely happy because this celebrations were not attractive without a snow. And it really happened that way. I don't know why, that whiteness was bothering me. I was eagerly waiting for your grandpa's return from work, but after the shoe store was ours and earnings were significant, I knew that Kristof would be working until late at night. Earlier, sometime in the evening, he brought a beautiful tree, something that we have never had before. Your father and Gertrude were very much happy. We all begun to decorate the pine tree with those few things that I kept in my box in order to reuse them every year. The largest work load around the tree was done by them, since I was preparing dinner. For that great night I made french fries and baked the turkey that I would enjoy with red cabbage and sweet nuts. Then I made a cake and boiled an apple compote. Over the table covered with a white cloath I placed two red candles connected with a silver knot, four white plates, a fork and knife. I placed the slowly prepared and churned food nearby those candles. The latest I brought at the table was a "Saher" filled with chocolate that everyone liked. Surprisingly, before we started to eat our food, curiosity and desire brought me closer to the window to see how the snow was covering my neighborhood.

-      There is a bad weather out there, - I said to myself and overwhelmed by longing I let the window drape down. Then I invited Kristof together with the kids to come closer to the

12

table. Their smiling faces I will never forget. It was the last night of Christmas that we awaited together. We were surrounded happily in our small table to pray to God for all good things gifted to us. We connected our hands with one another, closed our eyes and begun our wishes, this ritual was daily in my life and to all Catholics. Your grandfather always started first and then we continued, repeating word for word what he was saying: "God bless us and all these gifts, that we receive from your hands, through Jesus Christ our Lord. Amen."

For a few instants the room was covered by silence. As we kept our eyes closed and keeping our hands together, we called upon God to hold us united and happy during all our lives, just like this night. But when we said our latest prayer, God had slept and unfortunately did not listen to us. Immediately after the prayer we begun to take our food prepared under the savory tradition of Vienna. Johann and Gabriela after they ate the latest pieces of cake, opened their gift boxes served as genuine Christmas decorations on this night. Happy with everything, they laid down on the wooden beds, adjacent to our bed. It didn't take long and the kids fell asleep. I believed that there were no happier kids in the world than us. The kids were growing up every day. There was a great hope that a bright future was waiting for them until the moment when snow flakes appeared and destroyed our life. Melani was young, but remembered vividly the warm tears of her grandmother that were rolling over her face that was faded from a sorrow felt for her family members. The girl felt a endless pain for things that the old lady had gone through. She wanted to cry and did not know how to comfort her, she could only extend her fragile hand and with soft fingers wiped off her tears, that were rolling ruthlessly below her old cheeks. She kissed her grand daughter's hand and brought it close to her chest filled with suffering. Melani was her sole inspiration, was the only light that gave her a slight hope to live. In the blue eyes of the

13

little girl was looking at the eyes of Kristof and Johann, was looking at her round face and tall hair of the girl as well as the ambitions that one day she would become an actor.

- Oh, you are beautiful my love, - she wispered to the girl and continued to talk about the last night of their happiness that was ruined by the snow falling outside the window.

I felt that something wrong was going to happen. It had bothered not only my mind, but it was also attached after my body just like a snake, and kept me hostage all night. The adage "I am the end of your happiness" was torturing me. To no avail, in silence I tried to relieve myself, but without success. Ongoing worries were succumbing me everytime I came close to the window and whisking away the thin drape that separated horror with happiness.

- Snow, snow! This is swallowing everything, - I said to myself and shook my shoulders hurriedly from fear while encountered with the body of Kristof, whom I did not realize that he was standing on my back.

- What is going on with you? What is bothering you? – he said.

- Nothing, - I said to him. He touched softly my silky hair and slowly opened his powerful arms while comforting me on his chest with the greatest love that existed in his person, he almost knew that this was truly our final night. Gertrude had an insecure voice, but she did not articulate any word. She swallowed them.

-        We loved each other, my love. Among us there were no arguments. He was a

wonderful man, charming and beyond my beauty, he was superior. It was enough to look upon a woman and he could immediately attract every woman. His shoulders were marvellous and was attractive as a magnet. His bright white hair could not escape from the attention of every woman. Simply, he was a great person, a father, and a wonderful man.

You have inherited his light blue eyes, my dear. This is how Kristof was when I met him for the first time. He was the soul of my soul. A sibling soul of mine. The lips of the old lady were shivering sadly. She remembered the last night and her heart was falling apart. Having an old age did not fade her longing, pain neither love for him. She met them every day. Said good morning, good night, happy holidays my loved ones, and at the end she softly kissed the old photo she had never placed away from the furniture.

- Do you see this photography, my love! I have made this frame one week before Christmas.

Kristof had developed this photo tape with many other photos, but this was unique for him, therefore he gave me this as a gift for Christmas, when I saw him at the window. He invited me to sit on a nearby bed, brought two glasses of red wine and from this drawer he pulled up the photo of a medallon with our photo were grandpa, Johann and Gabriela were melted in it just like sweet angels.

- These are for you my love, - he said.

I took them, rose on my feet and hugged him with all my love. He had the same passion towards me with all that energy of love and said:

- I will love you during all my life, - My heart!

We remained together until the late hours after midnight. Wine glasses were poured one after the other and surprisingly we were not drunk, it was only propping our appetite to drink even more. We, both of us, that night experienced the eighth greatest marvel, - said the old lady and remained silent. Melani was eager to hear the rest of the story, however due to the girl's age, Gertrude did not see it fit to expand her story further, even though she felt it was necessary to continue thanks to a great love she had experienced that night. She stood up bowed and curved, turned a little on the left, extended her hand and grabbed the medallion from the cabinet drawer.

She kissed it in silence while looking beyond the window, she started talking with her dead ones. This ritual she repeated almost every day, but her niece was not afraid from the sorrow of the old lady when she said: - "Wait for me, my dear relatives. Even a little bit more time."

Melani felt often surrounded from the dead and willing to ask any questions to her grandmother in regard to her parents and aunt. The girl every day was looking at the pictures and meeting them through a photo. She knew that they were dead when she was a baby, but no one shared with her how they passed away. This is why Melani was suffering from absence of her parents just as the old grandma suffering for the whole family. She felt sorry for making her grandma go through such a longing, but she wanted to know more about the "Winter of the Century", consequentially she did not interrupt her. She was happy that after a long time Gertrude was determined to share with her the tragedy of their family. To make it easy for her story, she brought her a glass of water and a "Lindt" chocolate bar, that her grandma loved. The old lady, while afraid that the little girl would be shocked, could not speak any further, because the time had come. After swallowing a piece of chocolate that she was barely chewing, noted:

- We have spent many beautiful nights, but that night remained the best in my lifetime. I am not sure if we did sleep at all, I only know that when night was disappearing frightened from daylight, I woke up again disturbed and run immediately towards the window.

In that instant, a strenuous pain surrounded my neck and it spread across my body. What I saw, it froze me totally. Fear was powerfully running my brain, but the relentless snow, was eating my soul. I wanted to pray to the God of snow to command that, but I did not know was there a snow God? I had never heard of this. To whom could I pray? To whom could I beg? Who was listening? No one. Thoughts about Gods of nature, that I needed to reveal within myself

16

today more than ever before, were interrupted by Kristof when he suddenly stated:

-My love, the snow is over?

- No, - I said.

- Well, come to bed, it is still early.

- No, I said again, - I will turn on the heat to warm up our bedroom.

I was talking, but I could not understand why I was not able to escape from the window.

- Very well, I am coming to you, my dear. I saw she left aside her cover mantle and with two or three soft steps she was before myself, she became one with me, looking at the snow that was rising like a ruthless dinosaur and swallowing the city of Vienna. When she saw it, was shivering and spoke slowly:

- Look how beautiful it is. To be honest I love it very much. Look at how it is covering all the mistakes of the city. It is a perfect invader. Takes territories without any war. Its magic fully kidnaps you away and takes you into a surreal world. Isn't it true my love?

- Of course it is lovely, - I interjected with a lower voice and placed my head deep into his warm chest. The neck of your grandfather begun to relax after I embraced his body and was listening a few beautiful words for the snow that was driving me crazy. However, I felt that I had to escape definitely from the window and the marvelous snow of Kristof. I noticed that she was kidnapping it. I hated the snow and was jealous for your grandfather that was flirting with her. He was betraying me for the first time in my life. I slipped quickly while detaching myself from his hands and escaped offended. I wanted to cry so much. I wanted to pray the Goddess of Sun to melt the snow and to make it disappear once and forever from the face of earth.

- In winter I was searching for the sun. How confusing can it be, - I said to myself! Now he is far away and is warming up other continents. But, why is it important, where he was at that moment? I loved the sun at every cost, right in this room, exactly in this city. I also wanted to flirt with him, to possess him, to meet only with me, and then together the two of us would go against the snow, that was kidding with me and with its harmful white mantle was reigning the heart of Kristof. I was very, very naive! How come I could not understand that nature has its own laws and rules! Whether we like it or not, you are powerless to break them, even more so when you are a woman. In the legend a snow is said to be a powerful woman, but she is afraid from the sun. I am also a woman, but not a snow and of course I love the sun. Supported with my elbows over this table, with the head tucked among my hands, I did not ascertain that Kristof had turned on the heat spreading quickly across the room, warming up slowly my ice cold body and soul.

He was standing nearby myself, with two coffee cups that were unwrapping a great aroma. Placed them over the table, sat before myself and started to talk with his red eyes:

- Why are you so sad my dear? What is happening with you? Tell me please? You seem to be shocked!

At that moment I was traumatized, but he was a skeleton for me. I placed my hand over his hand, squeezed it very much so and had no courage to see it, I swallowed this coffee with the most bitter flavor that Kristof had ever prepared. With my lips covered by poison I saw darkness disappearing and snow dissolving, that was not stopping, just as my feeling that something that would happen could not be stopped. But, sharing this with him, his loud smile would be heard from our neighbors. I comforted myself, that it was only a revolution against the snow, created from my sick feeling, that was not leaving me alone. However, silence beyond the walls was crumbling. Some people had come outside their homes and started to shovel the snow, but were complaining on where to collect the snow, because its thickness had reached one meter and thirty centimeters. Old couples were looking from the window and would close them quickly. A man was swearing at the snow that had entered in his balcony and had covered his tree of Christmas and ruining it completely. The lady that was living in front of our building, was swearing at the snow. "Go to hell" she was mumbling as other neighbors were trying to clean up the streets.

- Therefore, I am not alone in this town who hates this evil whether, - I thought as I returned in the kitchen to prepare an egg omelette with a toast, I saw Kristof that had come nearby my radio and was listening the morning news. I was only interested at the latest part of news when the unpredicted weather over Europe would be shown. I was cooking with my ears on alert and waiting for the latest minutes of news when I heard soft knocks on my hallway. I headed to open the door, but your grandfather was much quicker than myself. The entrance of the apartment was covered by the old man living on the upper floor of the building. He explained to your grandfather that there was the risk of the top being crumbled due to high levels of snow. The age of the old man would not allow our neighbor to go up on top of the snow peak.

- If you don't do this, the peak will fall right away, - Said the old man to Kristof, begging and he left. Your grandfather closed the door and didn't promise anything but was evident that he had to work on the snow. For the first time, when the snow begun to cover the streets, I had never thought that something bad would happen. We exchanged sweet smiles among one another and together we sat on the table. We held our daily prayer, untied our hands, and started to have our breakfast. The room was reigned by silence. There was nothing heard with the exception of classical music in Radio-Vienna and tingling of plates and forks used to enjoy our breakfast.

Even more I was looking at the face of Kristof while enjoying my omelette. Although I felt sorry about his grim face, he was for me the most gorgeous man of my life. Even when we recently met, I had never felt such love for him, that I sensed on these moments. I loved him with all my existence, as I had known that everything, we were doing together would be the last thing.

- My dear, - I want to help you to clean the snow from the roof top.
- No, - he answered immediately. Kristof knew that I was afraid of heights.
- I do not need you. You take care of kids.
- Please my love, - allow me to help. Kids are behaving and they can take good care of themselves.
-     Obviously, - responded Johann! – I will take care of my sister. He opened his arms, brought closer his kids, kissed them on their heads and said:
- I am proud of you and I will always feel this way.
  The two happy kids, went a step back from their father's chest, looked into his eyes and responded:
- We are also proud with you Kristof! – Afterwards, they left. This is how they called their father in their happiest moments, and we were impressed in front of one another.

To talk about them was unnecessary. They were wonderful. The three of them were into one. You are very much like them, - stated the old lady to Melani, that was listening with great attention! – you are compensating my burned longing for the kids. The girl smiled to her grandmother, as the old lady was speaking.

- You wanted to help me, - is that true said Kristof while inviting me to follow him.

- I will be there, I responded without hesitation and hurriedly pulled up the empty plates from the table.

- Leave those over there Mom, - said your father! – I will do them.

- Thank you, - I said to him and went near Kristof that was looking to do something useful based on his abilities.
- We must wear thick clothes because is cold, - I spoke while standing inside a closet and looking for a wool jacket that my

mother had made many years ago. Although it kept me warm, I liked it due to a nostalgia that it embodied. I took the clothes, and, right after making a twist, in front of me appeared an attractive man and encompassed the highest peak of my heart.

A man looking as a capable alpinist, in the right hand was embracing powerfully two large shovels, and on the left hand was holding a thick leash. I almost broke apart from the desire to make love right there, in that moment.

- Are we ready Gertrude? – he said.
- Obviously, - I responded and while joking I did a military salutation before his huge shoulders.
- Yes sir I am ready.
- You are very beautiful, - he said.

I did not say anything, but only let him understand that I loved him so bad. At that time he pulled me swiftly and pegged within my lips without leaving me time to breath. Meanwhile, while he was taking the air from my lungs, I was absorbing the serum of love. Then he embraced me once more, robustly, and with eyes almost closed, he left me and went towards the door, and did not leave me to make another move, only to follow him.

Dressed in thick clothes, with shovels on hand, we went up the stairs one after another. Before entering underneath the roof, a shivering embraced my body. I did not know why I was embraced by a desire so that evil door would never be open. As I tried to insert the key, Kristof noticed that my hands were shaking. He took the key from me and made various attempts to open the old door, and the door of bad luck was opened. It was terrible, my love! Darkness had invaded the maximum and cold air shivered my soul that made me not to enter inside. Thunderstorm had made the snow and shingles into one, across the twenty-four hours and darkness was chewing the wooden pillars. I thought that wooden pillars were crying, screaming, were looking for help just like the souls of antichrist.

-   It is not called without a meaning as "the winter of the century", my dear, - Kristof said to me. He was looking for a light bulb that he thought to be somewhere hanging in the beams of the roof that were almost bending within. After finding the switch key, he turned on the light and placed it on a rusty nail. With all difficulties he was successful to remove the first shingle. I felt a great pain when the snow, mercyless, hit his beautiful face, but this did not stop him. Now he was on the top and pushing the snow at great ease, and I was standing below waiting for his signal to offer help. It was pointless. He had planned when I had to help. I could not wait any further and stood up without asking him. I pulled up my head on top of the snow. I was surprised. For a short time, Kristof was able to spread the snow from its highest peak up to a meter around the surface.
-   Do you need help? – I asked.
-   What do you want here? – he responded and was disappointed.
-   Still, - you don't need my help?
-   No. Go down, please, - he responded. – I will let you know when I need you. I still have a lot to do. First I will open a corridor on the four angles of the peak, starting with the last shingle that is touching the tent, all the way up to the top shingle, otherwise it is impossible to clean up this terrible snow.
-   He named it "terrible", - I thought once and silently inserted my head inside the darkness that was becoming brighter slowly. Almost immediately after me, he also descended.

- Do you need the leash? – I said again.

- No. You will be using the leash, but please hold on to this shovel, - he said. – I must remove two or three shingles here in the row before the last from the bottom.

- Ok, sounds good, - I said, and after a few attempts, he was successful to remove those shingles and the snow entered inside.

-   He is not giving up, - he spoke again and asked for his shovel.

Already with half of his body outside and the other half inside, he was pushing the snow with all it takes. I wanted to help him, but he was reluctant. Inside the roof, light begun to enter, and I continued for over thirty minutes to maintain the leash on my hands and waiting for Kristof to call me.

-   Minutes were going fast and I was very cold and was invaded by the monotony as I was listening the shovel that was shaving off the shingles, but also I was delighted to see that Kristof was throwing the snow at no mercy in the ground.

Suddenly Melani was looking at the grim face of her grandmother. She brought her a cherry syrup mixed with water and helped her to drink it. The girl was young, she never thought that her grandmother was at the end, but she begged her not to stop with her story. The old grandmother, while struggling, said:

-   Place more woods on fire because I am cold!

Then Melani became afraid that her grandmother would die. She could not imagine this could happen at the very same time when she was speaking, - to disappear from this life. She touched her cold hands that were over the blanket. They were very cold. Worried, she run towards the stove festered a few more wood logs and then went to bed, she opened her warm arms and brought close to her feminine chest, her dear grandmother. The steel was cracking.

Flames were covering the woods and warmth was spreading across the room, but the old grandmother was recovering the pink color on her face, distorted from suffering. She gathered all energy that was lost over the years and continued her conversation right where it was interrupted. Minutes were going and Kristof was not calling me. He would never allow me to risk my life, but one thing I was very sure, that he wanted me to stay close to him, because, had I gone away from that place filled with snow, in order to ensure that I was still there, he always said: "My love, are you cold? Hang in there a little bit more."

I never understood why he did not tie the rope in his body but instead he left it on my hands. That rope, right after his death has been hanging on that wooden beam and is still there. Everytime I see the ceiling and look at that, it makes me very wild. Always it seems to me that this rope turns into a chain and scoffs my eyes. How is it possible to suffer all these years and not pouring it on fire? Why didn't I cut it into pieces?

- Oh yes, why would you blame the rope since he never used it, - said Gertrure and continued with her tragic story, that happened to her.
- Right when I felt that kingdom of the world was falling apart and light was expanding all over, I listened a noise that bothered me. I rose immediately and run inside the beams after Kristof would be slipping below the highest peak and very fast would be falling in the

pavement. On those very few seconds I heard only the voice of extinction. Darkness embraced all my soul. My feet were frozen. I fell on my knees. I did not know what happened with him, But I had to stand up. Gathered my superpower strength and descended the stairs reigned by sorrow. I opened the door of the building and run fiercely. I did not know in what part he had fallen. In what place? I called his name. Although he was very close to me, I could not see him until I heard his painful voice. Oh God! He remained with a hanging body on the steel fences of the building. Was not moving at all. I requested help to those men that were cleaning up the snow.

They came right away. Gathered around him, carefully they lifted him so that he could get out of there. Even Kristof was trying to move, but his deep pains that had run into his back ruined his feelings. His hands and arms were totally lost, meanwhile in me every minute had turned into a century. My heart was made into pieces when I saw him half dead under the layer of snow that was melting on his grey face, saddly below the dark sky. With one hand I measured his pulse and with the other cleaned up the snow that was kissing his eyes. Was ticking peacefully and breathing steadily. Everything made me very sad until infinity. With a lot of difficulties those men pulled him out of there, and then entered inside and layed down slowly in bed the broken body of Kristof. Kids were very upset. Little Gabriela remained behind myself and started to cry. I asked those people to stay a little in the room until I could take away the children. I did not want them to see their father dying. I embraced them, went into the corridor, and rang the doorbell of my neighbor. Was a great friend of mine. I shared what just happened to me. She expressed her sorrow and kept the kids inside. Succumbed into sadness I expressed my gratitude and went right away towards my dearest person of all that was laying down. As I came near Kristof's bed, all men stepped back and left the house. Afterwards I sat next to him, touched his hand and I said:

- My dear, - Pardon me for leaving you alone.

He ascended his heavy eyebrows and looked at me. His face had the image of a pretty angel, but exhausted.

- Why didn't you call the Ambulance and the Medical Emergency personnel, grandma? – said Melani on those moments.

- What could have been done from the medical emergency service since all the streets were locked down, - Gertrude responded.

The snow was taking him from me, and no-one could do anything.

He was done, but his sadness and suffering were burning my soul. The only source of help was only church and my neighbor, who came nearby and said to me that I could go in the house of God to look for medicine against pain, even though the two of us knew that everything we could do was in vein. But what am I going to request when I go at the temple of God for myself, because his suffering were the source of my pain that I could not afford, - I thought and with a half dressed coat, I went through the snow that was grappling me up to my belt. I knocked in the door of honorable sisters. Sister Patricia came out, she gave me the medicine and expressed her condolencess that Kristof would be better.

- God willing, - I said to myself and held tightly the medicine in my fist while running under a cold wind that was burning my head. As I approached the building, I saw in the window a light turned on. My heart was beating hard. I felt that Kristof was almost leaving me.

Very quickly I ascended the stairs and with a tired breadth I entered inside. I almost fell when I saw that our neighbor was standing on his head that was burning. I dropped the medicine on top of the bookcase and came nearby his chest. I started to massage his untied hands. Then I placed my hand into his sweating front, I wiped his sweat and kissed his tears that were descending below his cheeks that were even colder than the freezing wind of that evening. He was moving only his lips that were the last attempt to say something that he could not say earlier. In his eyes appeared two peaceful oceans that were closed forever. His body was not as strong as the soul. He detached himself, descended in a fierce night that was called the "Winter of the Century". He was deceased forever meanwhile for me the departure of Kristof meant the end of the world. Too much pain! In my inner world I was screaming, was crolling, scratching my throat from calling out loud, cursing at the Gods of nature. The volcano of pain was exploding up until the destruction of every piece of my body, but I knew that he did not want me that way this is why all the pain I was hiding in silence. How didn't I understand up until that moment that with his eyes I had seen the whole world and when he closed his eyes, my eyes were both closed for ever.

Suddenly Melani was only looking at two blue tear drops of the old lady. Gertrude was vanishing, meanwhile the girl was misleading herself that her grandmother could stay for long. She wanted to know so bad for the father, for the others. She touched her hands just as two pieces of ice and said:

- Can I make you something warm to eat?
- No, - said Gertrude! - Please bring me a glass of water and put some more wood on the chimney because I am still cold.

After drinking a little water under the fire, she continued to speak:

- That night my dear, the three of us remained together for many hours in this room full of sadness. As the day was starting, I called all the people at the church. They came at 8 AM, they brought up his body, lifted him up and took the body in the funeral.

What about me, were could I go?

What could I do?

Nothing. Ruined, alone, I came to see through the window how the four men were lifting up on their arms my beloved husband vanished through the disaster of snow that was and continued to cover everything.

"May you go together with him." – I said to myself because I did not want to live any further.

Chapter 4

During those three weeks, my dear, night and day turned into one. I was walking as a lost person in the cold residence of Antarctica and even if they could bring the fire of all world in this room, my soul would not be warmed up. I was not drinking nor eating. My body was only in skin and bones, I was not accepting to lay down in the empty bed without my Kristof. I refused to accept that I had lost him forever, just as the kids were also refusing. I had told them that Kristof was gone and would not return anymore, but I did not allow them to see their father with closed eyes. They were young and I wanted to behold them away from the image of death.

However, they did not want to believe this. In silence, they were looking for their father in me. The closed mouths were grappling my fractured feet. Covered in sorrow, I had to collect that little strength and to embrace in my chest the remainder of my life.

The days were going by and I had not noticed that the weather was opening, and the snow was melting. In the third Saturday after Christmas, frightened, I was called by the servants of the church. They told me that in the next day Kristof would be burried together with a couple of other bodies that had been waiting due to a bad weather. A man on the other side of the phone said to me that everything was arranged in regards to the burying ceremony, because they had covered all expenses hoping to relieve even a little of our pain, their family members. Pain remains a pain I said to myself. However, I expressed my gratitude to that man. I hang up the phone and begun to cry. In the next day I woke up early and surprisingly I was in front of the window. Pulled aside the thin, transparent drape of the window and was looking at the peak of the church were the body of Kristof was resting. Vacuum was carving my soul up to infinity. The cold weather was hitting my body and I felt something that shook me up from top to bottom. I thought as

Kristof came behind me, embraced me just like years ago with his body, pulled his hand and touched my heart that started to hit hard while whispering in my ear: "do not worry my love. I am in front of you. I love you, my dear." I almost froze myself. Surprised I was looking around myself. When I tried to step away from the window the kids already were leaning on me.

- Mom at ten a clock we should go to the cemetery, - said Johann to me.
- Yes, - I said to my son that was looking to me with a broken heart.

I dropped again my view through the window and in silence I said: "I will also love you all my life, my dear." His absence was killing me together with the furious rain that was dancing over the glass. I had no idea what to do, except for embracing my kids under my arms and getting out of the main door. It was weird because the leash, used by Kristof earlier, was in my hands and it was intertwined within the feet of Gabriela, I wanted to take the leash with me and burry it together with Kristof. Instants later I changed my mind and decided to leave the leash at home.

It appeared that Kristof did not want that bloody thing. Perhaps had he been tied with that leash, he would have been among us now, alive. Then, I threw the leash nervously on the floor and headed towards the cemetery. I was walking exhausted on the street. Barely holding the hands of Johann and Gabriela, they both would grow up without a father. Rain nor tears that were coming together, mixed in my face were not stopping. They together were cleaning the streets of Vienna. On that moment Gertrude was covered by silence. She was all white, kissed again the medallion that was holding in her fist, wetted her slightly frozen lips with water, and with her right hand wiped the red faces of Melani.

- Yes, darling of grandma, - she said.

The doors of the cemetery were open. With thousands and thousands of graves, covered partially by snow, they were revealed in front of us. Right in the middle of graves was the old church, surrounded with oak trees older than the dead bodies. With all dark sky and the rain falling hard, the golden brightness of the peak at the church was blinding my eyes filled with tears. The street covered with cubes was leading us in the house of God. The door of the church had remained open. We entered and joined the sad family members, that were sitting on the wooden benches. The sad notes heard from the piano invited the priest, to come out of his Sacristy.

He stayed with his back turned a little towards the families present, did the cross, bowed in front of the statue of Jesus Christ, kissed the sacred book holding in his hands, and then turned his face towards us the living and before the dead people layed down next to the Altar. He did the cross again and started to preach the holy text. We the family members, filled by sorrow, were not listening anything, we only cleaned our tears and were covered by prayers. At the end of mass, the workers in the cemetery with mortuary uniforms, after the words of the priest "You were a dust and became dust", they came closely in front of the altar and took the dead bodies one by one, and we went behind them crying and succumbed into sorrow. Rain and tears were falling over the graves, my dear. The priest was sprinkling holy water above each grave and after him were walking the family members placing flowers. Latter on the cemetery workers with their musculous hands grabbed the shovels and swiftly were pouring the soil above the wooden body cases that disappeared slowly in the depth of earth. All men, exhausted from sorrow, were leaving step by step away from their loved ones, that were entering slowly in the chest of a cold soil, meanwhile from the inner circle of church were heard the fragile sounds of piano that faded more and more with the passing of time.

- Kristof broke my heart into two pieces, my dear Melani, - she said to the girl. I took the kids with my body soaking wet up to my bones and we walked in the street succumbed into sorrow. Finally, broken from sadness, I had lost the instinct of being a mother. I did not realize, that my kids' hands were not knited to my fingers up until I heard the squeeking of car tires that ruined the drums of my ears and hit furiously the body of my poor daughter into the wall of a nearby house.

Oh God, - I said!

Underneath the automobile I saw the long hair of my precious daughter Gabriela, that were turning into red color. At this moment, my hands were holding the bloody head of my poor baby. The rain was diluting the blood of my angel, but it could not dissolve the endless pain that soaked me in. I woke up in the hospital after one month, when everything was already all done.

The meaning of life was lost, at the time when your father died. He did not want to become a nazi solder. You stayed with me because that is how we decided. While attempting to escape he was killed together with your mother, somewhere in the middle of the Austrian – Swiss border. This was a pain that exceeded all pains. Melani, shaken by the stories of her grandmother, took the photo of her father from the furniture nearby, headed towards the window and disoriented was looking outside. Suddenly Gertrude was not speaking any further. The girl noticed that something was not right. She run immediately towards her bed. Called her many times, but she did not respond. Already in her grim face remained the stains of the untold words.

Chapter 5

The noise of squeaking wheels and sudden breaks frightened Melani, who opened her eyes and saw the vehicle that had stopped next to the cemetery. With its lights off, the driver was hoping to turn on the engine in front of gate number one of *SIMMERING*. He was trying to connect with the dispatcher but to no avail. It appeared that every telephone connection was broken. He went outside, looking at the road, but did not notice even the smallest move, not even a flashlight, not even a sign of life, meanwhile the snow and cold temperature were destroying our soul. He thought that the metro was broken from the bad weather and again entered inside, closed the door, while sad in his face headed to speak to the passangers that were worried:

- Dear passangers, I hope that everything will be fixed in a few minutes. Thank you for understanding! – he said and entered inside the cabin where he was struggling to turn on the vehicle. In metropolis Vienna was very unusual to have a metro car broken down and the affected passengers started to be afraid. Two couples, that were in love, came even closer to each other. Those seating alone pulled up their cell phones because they wanted to connect with the world outside of the metro car. Every attempt was in vein. The man under the deceptive light that appeared on and off in his cell phone's screen was looking at Ela that was not reacting at all. Such a decisiveness surprised him, meanwhile the Lady Cook had experienced such a disruption a few minutes ago, therefore she was silent and waiting on what could happen next. The blow, explosion of the engine was heard so loud and I even became deaf for a few minutes. People were screaming and grabbed the handlebars and tubes on the sides of metro car. No one understood what was happening, even the operator had no idea what was happening. The car had taken a velocity and was entering under ground. The fact that the ground was opening up and the metro car was descending, and descending was something observed only by the old lady and Ela. The large hole that was openned in front of them, reminded Ela the hole created in Guatemala. This phenomenon she had seen after a few years in a TV channel, were the program mentioned that such tunnels take you into hell. The two ladies understood that they were going into hell. They observed the layers of soil and rocks that were divided into two parts and with a lightening speed they were filled with snow as the famous sky cone. The unknown rocks were rolling and hitting across the many sides of the metal. The travelers were at risk of drowning. Ela, was confused, held the old lady very close to her chest meanwhile the later tucked her head in the chest of the girl and was quiet. Amid the layers of soil, they were looking at millions of skeletons that were ingrained in there. She had never thought how many people were underground. There were scenes that became deeply engraved in her head until the metro car hit furiously a sharp rock and the hair of the lady cook rose immediately. The two doors of the car were opened, and the two ladies naturally descended the metro car. Afterwards a surprising force threw the metro car over the surface full of snow. The equipment gear of the car became operational again. The engine was working, the lights turned on and faces of passengers begun to smile again. All of them started to applaud as if they were inside an airplane that was flying above the sea and risking falling at every moment. The Car operator, nervous due to the car that was broken apart, that lasted only a few minutes, was driving the metro car just like crazy as he approached the cemetery. The metro car disappeared together with its passengers in the darkness of thunder that was not stopping, but the fact that the two ladies were missing, no one had really noticed.

Chapter 6

Cold, obscurity. Someone was late. Perhaps him, themselves or the two ladies that were surrounded by fear and did not know were to go. They were silent sitting on the top of a rock and waiting.

-        "What are we waiting for" – said to herself Ela in the darkness that started to retrieve some light from the nearby light rays, that were coming from many sides. The kitchen Chef did not realize who had invited her or who had sent this old lady that had sneaked her head in her chest, at a time when they had not known each other. She was frightened from it and therefore she was looking for a solution. She looked upon the horizon and those images surprised her. Oh God, there are many people here! The roads of hell are frightening and horrific. Everything cannot be described. These matters cannot be described by any prophet, philosopher, scientist, writer, cinematographer or even by those people that have had a clinical shot down, not even myself looking with my own eyes, she was talking and was even more close to the old lady, meanwhile Melani was broken into pieces and pulled her head away from the girl's chest and almost became crazy when amid the steep mountains she saw those skeletons folded one after another. She was surprised with the largest stone on their right side.

The rock was a little lower than the peak were the ladies were staying and had almost the shape of a big canoe. Thousands and thousands of preserved skeletons, dressed in gold, were laying comfortably nearby one another. The ground of cemetery was bright, surrounded by thick and tall walls so that no one would get in and out and were sleeping in peace. They were not worried about events taking place beyond the steel walls. There were graves of royalty ranked with great taste, so that the old lady would better be laying down over there than here, but they were far away and she felt better in tucking her head within the blue mantle of the girl rather than go somewhere else.

Chapter 7

The sitting on top of sharp edges was really hurting those women. They were tired and their encounter with the unknown was making them struggle. They did not see no-one to go and help them, therefore knowing that they were risking their lives and unbeknown to them, who they were waiting for, they decided to depart. Afterwards Ela said to the old lady to not move and right after she begun to pull herself from her body, a few small stones started to descend below their feet. With her shaking body, she bent on her knees and was looking for a place were she could solidly, safely set her toes. Meanwhile she was cleaning the small pieces of the soil, her eyes went down, and her soul was shaken. With thousands of terrifying creatures, with their heads up they were looking at the women in silence. In the middle of a steel army, without the soldier that should have been as their head. He was on top of a black horse. The head of the animal was similar with the head of a rhino. The man was covered head to tows with black clothes. The mantel filled partially with metal was consolidated next to his body and his teeth coming out of his dropping lips were like those of Dinosaurs. The eyes of hatred were always attached to her. The head of a platoon as a wild animal was looking at Ela as if she were the destroyer of evil. Therefore, he wanted her heart alive. The meeting eye to eye amid the good and the bad was reflected. He was screaming and beating his chest together with the ugly creatures, engulfed into darkness, because the girl would belong to him. Everyone wanted from Ela the flesh and blood that was flowing in her veins. Even the good one was looking at the leader of evil in the eye. Distance was not stopping the lady to see the eyes that were pouring hatred. Frightened, she started to mumble "O God, help me! Oh God, please, help me!" – she said again. But she did not hear anything. He was sleeping. At that moment, the ugly headed towards the disoriented, confused girl and tried to climb on top of the rock. Surprisingly once they were in contact with the rock, they would dissolve it. Ela did not know that inside this sharp rock were enclosed hundreds and thousands of good people that were living with the light coming, on and off, from the Holy Spirit inside the fortress without a gate. They would be liberated only from the good ones, from a heavenly soul that did not belong to the world of evil and only in the new year's night would resurface. For this reason, the mother of peace had chosen Ela. She was the only one to do this with a few predetermined conditions. If the first Sun rays would fall on the earth and the kitchen chef would remain in the world of hell, the living people would loose their man, and the good ones that were dead would be lost even more because everything is coming back. The mother of all, who did not approve neither action, sent her Holy Spirit in a Dove's shape. The white bird was hitting his wings before the ladies and told them, to remove the wood log below their feet. The girl was not listening to what the man with wings was saying. The fear that she would be falling in the hands of evil animals, frightened her, but also gave her strength to remove the small stones around her feet, up until her hands met with stone plaque as big as a gramophone disc. She stopped and after she touched the circled stone, closed her eyes and ears, and pulled it up until her sweat was wettening her hair. Quickly the two women started to scream. Both of them were shaking over the rock's peak that was swiftly opening and the round stone surface was dropping them from one stone to another, right until they fell in the ground, were powerfully hit in the ground and lost their feelings.

Chapter 8

Ela was coughing and her nose was filled with dust. She was barely breathing. She barely could open her heavy eyebrows. Ela was exhausted as if she had fallen from the sky. Everything was coming around her. She felt like a dead person. Made a circle slowly on one side and tried to wake up, but her body was not responding. She descended again on her back, closed her eyes and with her two hands she pressured her head so that her mind could stay in place. Remained like that for some time because her feet needed a break. When she calmed down a little, she brought up her head and laid her elbows down to see where Melani had fallen. With twisted bones she directed her vision beyond herself. With the exception of the old lady that was standing laid down adjacent to her and was accompanied by interesting faces. Humans like skeletons gathered around those women that were smiling, were licking and encouraged to touch them. Ela knew that she was not anymore among the living people, but she could not understand this world of the underground.

- Is it true that the dead have surrounded us? But what are we searching over here and what do they want from us? How come the dead can smile? I cannot believe this, - she said.
- Hey you? Laughing with me? – she talked to them resting on her elbows. She turned her head and smiled as much as her voice confused that large crowd gathered around her.

Filled with the smiles of dead people, she looked towards the light that was by far warming her up and looked at the closed walls. She wanted to satisfy herself in thinking that she had descended in a castle of abandoned kings, but inside there were living defeated foreigners coming from evil times, and that she could go away when she wanted. Then, to calm down her eyes, she looked at the ceiling. In the dome of

castle, she did not see a piece of art that would attract her, she simply saw a few graphs scrapped were one could see forgotten saints and crosses, almost invisible. "Perhaps it could have been a church", - she thought and extremely tired she got completely lost in the ceremony of mass that was held outside her city at noon of deceit. That day full of passion Ela sat in the front row and wanted to follow the mass with great interest. She started to play piano. Men were standing on their feet and from the preparation room there exited four servants with long white skirts that were following the top person of faith. Later he came out dressed in the holy cover, walking greatly towards the altar. The Cross prepared with cordons of Gold, was ascended greatly above his chest and on both sides of his lungs, and the soft angels tied around the bottom lines of the skirt, made even more glorified the envoy of God. The pastor came nearby the marble that had disappeared with a white cover, stitched as well with crosses. The cover of shoulders was brightened by the candles placed on both sides of the table. On the right side of the priest was shining the gold cup. Over that was carefully placed the clean cotton towel, that could be used only by the priest. The cross as well was dominating the Altar and was decorating the house of God. Ela, lost in the greatness of this cross that was adding a meaning to holy mass, was trying to count how many times she had touched the cross with her wet lips. She was doing this thing only when she had trouble in school. Almost always one day before taking exams she was falling asleep before the altar, she was doing a prayer, kissing it with a lot of love and relaxed, that God would help her the next day to go home. As she tried to number those kisses, the priest had raised his hands towards the people and with a dominant voice stated:
- Let the Glory of Jesus Christ.
- Always for life, - responded the warshipers.
- In the name of the Father, Son and the Holy Spirit. Amen!

The church was echoing, meanwhile Ela suddenly forgot to rise in her feet and follow the mass. She was focused on the body of the Holy Lady, that appeared to be talking with her. The lady with a small body that gave birth to the King of Earth and Sky made it trustworthy that she was present and was blessing it. However, once she withdrew her eyes from the blessed one, encountered the picture that ruined her faith. Inside the multicolored frame, the painter had revealed all apostles, loved and overly happy, except for one that was different from the others.

He was breaking her image of trust. A man with a brown color skirt, with the leash tied around his body was holding the cross with his head laying down. He was inclining and depending on it. He did not feel sorry on what kind of position the wood log was standing, on which Jesus Christ had been pouring blood. Ela did not like this image. Inspired by the curiosity to know from whom when it was painted and what is the desire of the artist to express in it? As she was struggling with the meaning of this drawing the wholy book was being read, people were singing great songs and through their hands they said to each other: "Peace be with you! Peace be with you! Peace be with you was leaving slowly and it turned into the meaning of a huge rock. Before her face was emerging the shadow of a woman, and a skinny hand extended on her was making her upset.

- This is Tana, - she responded. The kitchen chef was not brave to avoid her vision from above, but she went walking, layed down, with her feet and hands, quickly until she encountered a wall with her head. At that moment she grabbed the rocks, stood up, came around and with eyes beyond the people, she was looking everywhere to find the door. She did not see any exit. Layed down in the well carved stone, for a moment she bowed her head, because the lady dressed in black, with disorderly hair covering her face, was frightening her. Already the two ladies were standing in front of each other without exchanging their eye contact.

Ela beyond herself was hearing the crowd of people – turned into skeletons – as they were whispering, meanwhile Tana was not making a move. She had a strong character and had plenty of time to wait. She never thought to give up neither explain why she had become this way? Her own secrets she wanted to share at the right time. Without any words and with the head resting over the chest, she requested to the girl only to hold her hand that she was holding for much longer in the air, meanwhile Ela while ignoring further the lady standing in front of her, continued to see the others that were beyond this lady.

Humans, like skeletons, gathered in there, started to like them, because they appeared friendly. The faces and all sorts of dresses surprised her. Among them there were some people dressed with cheap clothes, with suits and expensive shoes, some others were covered only with a blanket, the young ladies with bridal dresses sprinkled with mud and the kids with clothes full of colors, were tucked in the breast of every women. Surprisingly, those dressed in expensive clothes, were walking with their bare feet, and holding their brand-new expensive shoes next to their chest so they may not get ruined. In all this confusion Ela was bothered by some men that were pretending to be kings. "The kings" were naked and without a crown. Someone had taken off their clothes and golden crowns, meanwhile they were rolling now through the feet of some youngsters that were entertained while playing across that space. "The kings without a crown" did not even have their head. Their dried skulls were placed over their knees, skinny knees, and were longing blaming the holy for their fate. The lady cook felt bad for them, but her friendship she wanted to share with people that were not bragging. They grabbed her heart.

She was looking at their bodies, being dissolved the same. They seemed so skinny, so their clothes kept being pegged on their bones. Women with long hair, and men with short messy hair, that the soil had given them the color of crude silver, were sitting close to Ela and smiling, commenced to beg her.

- Please madam, - do this for the deceased, for us the poor, for us the forgotten, do it, please!

The calls begun to awaken not only the cook, but also the young guy with the image of an orphan angel that was sitting over the stone, carved on the right side of Ela. In the skinny hand he was keeping the wooden violin and was looking for the change of living girl. Perhaps he was the only one that was observing how she was moving her hand towards the cold girl and then was pulling her again. The Violinist understood that she was missing the guts, courage, and needed support.

-The Song "My heart is your home" will give her courage, - said the young boy with a violin and supported his chin above the king of instruments, he placed the small fingers over the chords and created the sounds that gave courage to the girl. Ela was looking at the violin stick that was magic, the ladies singing sweetly, Melani that was giving courage behind her shoulder and slowly was becoming a simbiotic connection with fear. After taking courage from everyone, she moved her eyebrows quickly over the frightened eyes and while looking at the cold woman that was not pulling out, she squeezed her skeleton hand. They both were frightened and became scared. The contact with ladies was surprising them! Death died. Tana with her head resting over the chest was gaining life. Below the skin her heartbeat started to become even weaker and then picked up fast. Her blood vessels were becoming warmer, blood was steaming across her veins and flesh was chilling. She turned again into a person of flesh and soul and transformation into a living creature made her feel sorry for the deeds that she had done. Even though her eyes could not see the life beyond her hair, she felt it, and enjoying on every part of her grim body. She was happy with truth that she was living once again, meanwhile the crowd of skeletons stopped their song. They sensed life, indeed.

-Hey people, smell of life is here! – screamed one person.

-Life? – said the others! – We also want this, and headed towards the living girls, to touch them.

Tana and Ela now had their shoulders together, their hands extended were spreading the breadth of life without any struggle. Women and kids were the first ones that were taking on their hands the most precious thing and running towards their chieftains. The brave one, sitting over the stone shaped as a royal highchair, was standing with his face turned towards the wall. Undisciplined and full of doubts that his army was reviving, he was not reacting. Ela, while looking at how strict he was, departed towards the trenches.

- Stop, - said Tana! – the knight for the foreigners is cruel.

- He has no need for life?

- He has never died, - responded Tana, - but however he needs to live.

- Sounds good, where was this person born that makes him eternal?

- In the soil of eagles. They have kept him alive.

- And what does this mean? She raised her hand to keep away Tana's hand that was cutting her path. At that moment, the holy spirit penetrated through the thick walls and standing in the air, talked to Ela. This time she started to hear it well.

- Only the living people can relieve from this darkness those man that are punished for a crime that was not committed, - was talking the bird! – Be advised that your time is contingent. And your other group can help her, so you should act quickly, please. Find the exit. Open the door of salvation! In this moment Ela understood who had kidnapped her from the world of the living and brought her here, who had filled with the dust of courage such a decent and timid woman in order to fight evil.

- Hey what are you waiting for? Act fast, - started to talk the white dove surrounded by a holy light and disappeared on the direction where it came from.

The two ladies were staying face by face. They did not have the slightest idea how to open the gate, only requested to the people to gather in the middle of the ground and set free the walls. They turned their hands into fists and with the edges of their fingers they started to softly hit the rocks while listening carefully, inch after inch how was the sound of closed walls. The tracking did not show any sign of exit.

- There is no difference, - said Tana, she was nervous and was looking at Ela that was not stopping on the other side ot the tower.

- Search, gather information, do not stop because there will definitely be an exit, - she started to whisper.

- I have never searched before, - said the girl with her head bowing down. – Perhaps had I tried something similar I would not be dead.

- Evil is ingrained badly in this place, - reminded Ela with her desire to set her free from the feeling of guilt and set herself apart from the fear of failure. They could not find a single hole. However, both were not giving up. When the minutes were almost over, the voice of Melani started to sound:

- Hey ladies, - there is the road that will take us outside.

The two ladies run towards the round stone where there was standing the Violinist Flo. They pulled aside the young Flo and pushed the stone with all their efforts. While fighting like gladiators in Roman arenas, they managed to roll over that piece of rock not so big, but surprisingly heavy.

After moving the stone, before them appears the infinite abyss. People over joyous, filled with life gathered over there and were looking at the whole, meanwhile the girl with her face covered was polishing the weak shoulders of the lady cook. And then went before the people and said:

-We left the curse behind us. This is the first victory against the bad ones. All of them were loud and said:

-Hurrah! Hurrah! Hurrah!

In those instants, the breast of Tana exploded from happiness. She filled up her lungs with happiness and was the first one to insert her right foot on the hole. After she stepped on something strong she also went forward with her left foot, and just like a kid when starting to make the first steps in life, she departed over the steps of stone. Everyone went after her. The same actions were taken by the staunch and brave leader. Freedom was more powerful than his pride. He tucked his sword inside and was following those disappearing below the unknown earth.

The deeper they entered the lesser was their fear. The two ladies, like powerful fighters, but with skiny hands, were entering in the ruins that stretched one after another. The frightening roads were taking the people below, lower, and lower, until they came out in a wide garden with a well ignited space. They stopped to rest. They were tired but happy because it was their best moment in their lives after death. People were still enjoying life and freedom although evils of hell had taken them away earlier. Only Ela had nothing to celebrate. She was not missing anything, so she was very busy with the city in front of her. Landscape was saying many things. Ela was looking surprisingly the destroyed walls beyond the bridge and did not want to believe it.

-Oh, I have lived in the suburbs of this city, - she whispered with surprise and saw the bridge that was separating her from the ruins.

-Yes! This is the bridge that I was crossing every day when going to school. I want to enter. What is there to be feared of? I have passed a thousand times on these areas. Day and night without any fear and departed to walk over the cubic stones of the bridge that was built many centuries ago. Below her feet, below the tall stone, she saw the riverbed where she had often been sweeming in the warm days of summer. She took a deep breath to enjoy the smell of water mixed with iodine just like earlier. She was deceived. The river had run out of water. On the sandy surface she was looking at the remnants of the city and here and there she found sceletons of a dead animal. Her silky hair in waves over her face was touched by the tears of pain. The girl had experienced the ruthless fighting in her city, but she could not accept that today, after so many years, her birthplace would be succumbed deep at the bottom of inferno.

Why, God is happening in this way?

Tell me what has happened?

Please, give me an explanation?

She wanted to ask, but she remembered that God was sleeping. Even if God would not be sleeping, he was not going to say anything, because the almighty would never bring obliteration to his earth. This was done by someone else. She wanted, with all her depth, to be blind at that moment. She felt very sad. She could not cross the bridge. She was not capable to face misery and poverty on the other side of the bridge.

Tana with her head down was joining the sorrow of Ela. Reaching nearby her, she seized her shoulder and started to walk together inside the empty city. The feet of both girls were drenched up to their knees in dust. In the middle of earth particles was hiding the tabloid that was hanging and shaking at the entrance. Ela grasped it with her hands and streaked the dust carefully. Taking away its dust, she was able to read only the first three letters *"Gj-a-k"*[1]. She pulled back in deep grief. But where are the last three letters? Who took them away? No, it is not true that this is my town. It was not like this when I left this town! She yelled with great sadness and cussed at the time and people of her world. With

---

[1] The word for "blood" in Albanian language.

her hair falling she was not speaking at all. Ela was following from behind her friend that was going through up the street. She let her get out the frustration, to pull out her nerves that were blowing her head.

-Is the church, - Ela spoke again as she was asleep.

-Where? Was heard the voice of a revived girl.

-There, on the right, at the wooden gate with a steel cross.

-Yes, yes, this is the church, responded Tana frightened even more from the quietness that was reigning the city. She did not like this silence. Was afraid of the sudden frightening surprises. With her eye was controlling the abandoned cities, meanwhile the lady cook entered in the kitchen and she came out the same as when she entered. Only that she almost vomited all her stomach out.

-What is happening? – asked Tana that was going after her. – Hey, tell me, - What do you have?

-Oh no! Do not! How is it possible? How? - And she put her hand on her mouth to not talk again. No, she could not remain silent before the crazy disgrace in the house of God.

-The church is filled up with naked people, -she said. –They were praying before Saint Mary; her eyes were pouring blood. Do you know what these idiots did? They were looking at me and then started to laugh while letting me know that somehow they liked my blanket and wanted to be covered with it, - she responded and she left hurriedly and confused towards the direction of the mosque in order to escape from the nakedness. Decided to close herself in there. She wanted to relax. She entered inside and closed the door. What she saw was: worshipers were grabbing themselves and were fighting among each other.

-Oh God, -she said! –These people are not praying, but they are fighting! With their hands connected to their knees she was looking where was their muzzle!

-Yes perhaps, but where are their eyes? She was talking brashly to herself. Her ears were echoing and energy was letting her down from sorrow. She could not hold herself anymore. The inner walls of the mosque were becoming smaller in her eye pupils and right when she was ready to hit someone, a powerful hand of a man pulled her with a magnetic force and she could not understand anything with the exception that she saw the face of Tana over her face.

-I am looking at your eyes, - she said with an abundant voice! – Hey, do you understand what I mean? I am looking at your mouth, cheeks, - the lady cook was saying and pulled up her hand to feel her purple eyes. Tana quickly unrestricted her dark eyebrows. Pressed furiously her cheeks, concealed her head on the chest and was moving without any control. Up until now no one had seen her face. On that day when she convicted herself with assassination, terrible evil that wanted to bring her with even more immoralities, gifted her some ultraviolet rays, giving her power and energy so that through the eyes of the girl, she could destroy the good men and their chieftain that were isolated together for centuries.

- My eyes can kill, -said the girl with her unrestrained hair! – did you know this?

- No, - responded Ela.

-Yes, they are destructive. I am the destruction of myself, but not your's. Not for the good one. For this reason and for the terrible work that I did, I condemned myself to keep my head hanging and will keep it like this until I take vengeance. The one who gave me a courage for bad, the bad one will kill him. One time I let my soul to make a mistake. That will never happen again. What would happen if those cursed knew that the chieftain is free today and I am his contrary? What will happen, hey? Inferno will explode.

Tana was much more furious than the flames coming from her mouth. Her bones were cracking, shattering below her black layer and her torso was errupting fire. Her blood vessels almost exploding.

The disoriented people were holding the sorrow of the girl and Ela that was mixed really bad. She felt the need for the counsel of someone else, because the unlimited furry that existed inside herself could have been fatal for both. She was not prepared to soften the resentment of this nature, came closely and said:

-Did you forget, that: "we are the life of others"?

The lady cook was not trusting herself. With a few words she turned her into normal. The lady with ultraviolet, after being shaken in her body, took her hand, strangled tightly and the two, in one voice together called: "Everyone against the bad ones." The echo of the voice covered the whole city. The youngsters coming from the Park of Freedom, were holding weapons on their hands, and pursuing the voices of women. Where they had found the guns, they were the only ones to know it.

-Weapons in the world of the dead? – questioned Ela! – What? Why, can the dead be killed? Even with a weapon?

-Hell knows overall the language of war and punishment, often it is even done without justice, - said Tana.

-But I need a victory without blood, - said the cooking lady.

Is known that women do not want victims, but the peace lovels without weapons would not make their feet, because the bad only know the sword.

Then the girl went in the streets of the city and was looking the preparations that were done by the warriors. Was looking for her birthplace that was destroyed and hanging wipes through the doors of institutions. These wipes meant cultures that were not part of her tribe. The fabric drapes with many colors that were waved through the air of broken freedom, were inciting fire in her soul.

In silence she was begging the cloud that was rising towards her, to cover these fabrics and other parts of the burned earth. Broken hearted, she left Tana to deal with the soldiers and left towards the center of town. Before stepping in the heart of the early town full of galleries, appeared a red line that cut her walking path. She went backwards confused. Then she gathered her energy and said:

-I will step exactly onto this line, which is like a border area that is guarded well. No one can stop me from crossing it. And without thinking much, she placed her foot over the line with blood color. In that moment something unexpected happened. The city started to wake up. Statues, fallen walls, houses, trees were covered by rotten vegetation and everything that was dead; started to get the life back in the city. Darkness was disappearing slowly, and the light was returning blossoming flowers. Her heart started to beat even stronger as she was looking at the women leaving their typical clothes and uniting with men. They were sharing stories with the soldiers, filled with pain, how they were abused from those knights with dark souls, who grabbed with violence their kids to do a brain wash and then turn those kids against their proper fathers. The women begged the soldiers to take them with themselves.

Ela surprised from the people, was walking through the streets with a delight. Since her time when she was in the nadirs of earth, she had never felt this joyous before. She was happy on how the ugly would turn into a good one. Delighted, she left that part and started walking in the cobblestone street that was taking her in the hills of the city. Step by step she came at the top of the hill. In there she was led by thoughts that she was holding a piece of land in her open hand palm. While grabbing her fist, she sat down and thought how big the force of a woman is, when she is determined to hit the ugly and evil with love! At that minute, her hair and cheeks were wet. She was the only one to know if these were the tears of happiness or the drops of rain that were falling continuously. Tana was helping the soldiers to get ready, let them to work and later she went after her, because of feeling that she was crying. Tana felt bad, then she came close to her under the rain, she entered underneath the blue blanket of the lady cook and whispered in her ear:

-You are a magic soul. Righ were your foot is stepping in, there is always life.

-Not only me but all women, - responded Ela and they together hugged each other under the powerful thunderstorm that was covering the hill. Tana and Ela did not know that from the three wisdoms that Holy Spirit had given to them, two of them were over, but happy they headed upon the streets eroded from ancient history through the rain that was dropping on top of people, weapons and over the bloody city. With the heavy mantles from rain they were attacking those peace lovers to hide behind the oak tree after the thunderstorm was over. Above the wooden log, in the thick branch that was extended as a black shadow on top of the women's head, was standing up Flo, who was trying to fix the messy chords of his wet violin.

-Look, look, through the rain he is thinking of playing the instrument? Work of kids, - said Tana to her and with her head up she asked the young boy in case he was able to find somewhere the chieftain.

-    "I am behind all of you", - his voice broke the space.

Men and women turned their heads towards him and were looking at the forgotten knight that was standing before them, meanwhile the two women remained behind everyone. Ela stood up on top of her fingers. She wanted to see the face of the man whose voice reached her, but in front of here there were many people and it was unbearable to get closer.

-Very good, - she said to herself, - you will see him next time. And opened her ears to see what the man was saying.

-My dear people. We are all free today and full of life while expressing our gratitude to a woman, that I have not met yet. Ela opened her ears even more.

-The great monsters want her, they want her heart alive, but this will not happen. The greatest threat for the girl is if she will not turn to where she came from before the morning light. For the second threat we will learn later. This city is becoming ever more unsafe for everyone, this is why we have to leave, she said quietly.

In those moments the resonating voice of the brave man was softened by the walks of the horse and the soft horse's reaction voice behind the shoulder of Ela, awakened her curiosity to see who was behind her? She vibrated just like the first time. She knew him. Was the man with a horse that had made her sad in the Schwarzenberg Plaza. The prince saw the mistress softly and like a real gentleman came close to her, bowed, kissed her hand, and excused himself for frightening her.

-As a compensation I have brought to you three horses. Please, accept this gift, he said with his lips full of sweetness. The girl did not speak, but she came closer to the horse and caressed his white skin. When she went to hug the knight that had made her sad, earlier, he was lost already in the middle of the reborn crowd that was cheering him:

-The good ones will fight, because they want peace!

Then she rested her head in the neck of the horse and very excited continued to knit the horse's hair that was ready to stage Ela on his shoulders.

Chapter 9

The four fighters gathered around the chieftain were talking about how to escape before arriving those that were pursuing them? One of the boys said that he knew a secret exit on the southern side of the city, but the path was very dangerous, especially for men. He was saying that they needed to pass a river called as the River of Nausea. He was saying: "It is not so deep to get stuck inside" – but, he said, "if a drop of water touches the thirsty lips of over ten men, then the river waves will swallow the women and kids."

-It does not seem easy to me, - responded the knight! – how are we expected to know about those people that want to plunge their head in the "River of Pleasure."

This is how he named it on that moment and placed his hands inside his snow-white hair, and after a while he said:
-I have an idea.
Men were listening to him.
-We must beg the people to not touch nor sip a single drop of water until we all have passed the river, then if anyone wanted, not only he can wetten his lips but also can take bath in the river. The brave man was hoping that while offering a little support to men, would be successful in safeguarding the majority or all of them. Therefore, the four men spread the news among the other ones and all of them departed towards the sinful fluid. The row was becoming long behind the brave man, going towards the pond – river of pleasure.
Men succumbed in the river remembered the words of the knight and submerged until their stomach in the poisonous liquid, were passing very well one after another. Even those that were extremely loving the liquid, were licking their lips, but were not touching it. Ela and Tana were walking behind the row. Were afraid that they would not make it through the water of vice, therefore they did not think about it. They were talking to Flo that they wanted to learn the parts of his violin and the young man was explaining to them until the river started the waves. The girl with her head down stopped immediately. After the death she had become a specialist of surveillance. She knew all sensations.
- Bad soldiers are behind us and are coming with an intrepid speed, - she said! – they will get to us faster than we think. The river for them is not a problem, because they do not drink this liquid. To escape from this, we must hurry up and our leader does not know that the army of rhinoceros is here, - started to talk again the girl like a violet.
-But how can we tell him, - since he is far away?
They were worried and looking at the people that were going towards the mountain that could be seen from there.
-I know what do to, - Ela jumped from her place. – the word is faster than us or no? Me and you will inform those

standing before us and let each one of them inform the one sitting next to them that bad knights are coming. They did this. The news went from the end to the begining of the line, touching on the ears of everyone. Until the priest became aware, he pointed his eyes towards the mountain.

It was the only possibility to come out safely. Then he ordered the soldiers to place the elderly and kids quickly in the chest of wood logs. But, as they were coming closer to the Oak logs, the brave gentleman was becoming ever more dubious to be hidding there. He felt that something was not good in the mountain in front of them. And disaster was happening. From the tall wood logs were coming white clouds and going towards them. Now powerful dust clusters were entering mercilessly in the bodies of good soldiers. The purpose of the mountain was to explode the lungs of these people full of life, but it appears that the God of mountain was mistaken.

The air shaped into clusters that he was hitting towards the soldiers was turning into a greater source of life. Ela was looking at how the air was entering through the clothes that were almost transparent. First, they were vibrating slowly and softly, inflated and then as if you were sniffing with a vacuum, they were desinflated up to getting pegged to the skin filled with the ashes of happiness. The air particles that were entering inside peoples' lungs, was strengthening even more their respiration. With a heart broken and failed, the lord of the mountain was talking something that only his property could understand. He raised his hands in space, collected the turbulent wind, and spread it across the people spreading it like a fire dragon. The wind particles were coming here and there around the people that were bowing down, who were expecting to be pulled up by the wind and to be sent no one knows were. The screams of kids were even louder than the neigh of the horse. The eyes of the living were shining in the night very much so surprised and unexpected occurrences were not stopping. Soldiers in panic, together with wild animals, were leaving the soil. As it appeared, even the wind and air were doing the opposite effect of what the lord of the mountain wanted. Everyone was staying over the surface of earth on a few inches. The ruler of woods failed again. Very much disappointed he pulled rapidly the wind. The peace lovers hit the ground and the chieftain above the horse was not expressing his worry that had engulfed all his body. On the other hand, Ela was not interested to know what was happening around her. The air and wind were not something new for the girl. There was something more powerful that was bothering her. She wanted to know even better that man sitting on top of the horse. The girl was burning from the desire to see the turbulent face of the Braveman that almost killed her even before the war started.

- "From the eyesight of the knight you could be blind", - Tana had told her, but now the lady cook was not willing to wait longer. She had no fear to see him. Then she releaved her body slowly, raised her head and not far from herself her eyes encountered the man with a tall body covered by a red mantle that was touching the knees of the horse. In the land of mantle, together with his silver hair, was waving the double headed black eagle, that was covering his wide shoulders. The image of this knight was tumultuous in her heart. Now she understood why she had pressured herself to know that person.

-No one can stop me, - she thought! – I have no reason to be scared. Immediately pulled the leash of the horse and with the back of the boots was poaching the rear parts of the animal. Very abruptly was found before him.

The brave knight was shaking as someone asleep from the crazy dreams. The bitterness that had erupted suddenly inside the body of this man brought fire to the eyeballs that even the stones were afraid. The girl was cut in half, was extinguished before the feet of man. On that moment, the unexpected darkness that came from the mountain totally covered the woman's body and hit the Knight, whose body was almost paralyzed. Similar hits were experienced even by the other ones. Before the darkness that was expanding unceasingly, they were weak. They could not handle it. The sources of darkness just like cannon shells were making the people almost motionless. The chieftain was losing his army, and this made him sad beyond limits.

- My burning eyes cannot be closed on any circumstances, - screamed and the furious light that was coming from his eye pupil was keeping alive the people behind his shoulder. Darkness was fighting fearlessly with light, and the fire of man's eyes was dissolved quickly. Then he pulled out his sword, raised it up while screaming towards the mountain with all his voice.

- Leave me a path. I must not end here.

But the ugly men of darkness were celebrating while hitting with their fists even more the chieftain that was worried, and the army of the bad ones was coming closer. The vibrations of earth and hearts shaking together with the dust had taken under control those reborn people. Confusion was ruining everyone. They did not know were to go. They were exhausted up to being exhumed. Ela was brought up from earth and remained leaning over the scared horse's body. Darkness and dust were bothering her. She was coughing but was much stronger than the others. She saw Tana and then the brave knight. The two were confused so much as they were roving around alone. When the hopes of salvation were becoming extinct, she was boiling. She strongly grabbed the leash of the horse and without even thinking the consequences she headed towards the mountain. Surprisingly, the mountain was cut in half. The tops of the oak trees touched the ground. Bowed they were opening-up their arms before the girl, opening the path for her. The courageous cook: was pushing the horse even more, to enter quickly in the open heart of the mountain. At the moment, she turned her head to see where the chieftain was. He was going after her. Then Tana was going after her with one thousand of peace lovers. Darkness was hiding behind the big mountain. Before entering in its stomach Ela closed her eyes and was lost among the paths of trees, that tested the good ones three times. From that moment she was not seen from anyone except for oak trees with their open arms that did everything to let good people pass without any harm. The eyes of untouched earth were looking at the bad guys filled with hatred that were falling in the body of darkness without asking it. With swords they were cutting every obstacle that was coming before them. They were never so close to the brave man's army, therefore they entered deep and deep without thinking what they were doing. Before everything they wanted the heart of Ela that was donating lives. They were not worried about the lord of mountain and for his disapointment. Even, they underestimated the destruction of the tree branches along the way and were bending so that those branches would not be ruined, until they would receive the order from the king of longevity. The God of earth, that was grabbing everything that he wanted to occupy, when he became confident that no-one from the good ones was left without a farewell, made a loud voice. Suddenly the wooden branches stood up and the corridors were closing quickly. Through the street, were they could walk earlier, now were opening endless ravines of abyss that were swalloing everything. Roots were coming from the earth and were turning into snakes that were tying the bodies of bad ones up until their total fracture of bones and feet, and then these bodies were thrown in front of the wild humans. The bad ones were experiencing destruction. Violence was not the corridor that would take them towards victory, so they had to withdraw and find another way that would be convenient to them.

Chapter 10

The exhausted soldiers were taking a break in the forsaken field, that was stretching before them. The girl with a violet colored eyes came close to the knight that was still angry about the war that he had with the mountain and with his head leaning on the chest he wanted to say that the Girl of Life is ready to die, but he did not see the face yet. From the white beard that was remaining hanging in the air, he observed that disappointment was still not over and if he would say it immediately something foolish could happen. Then, timidly she slowly placed her hand over his wide shoulders. The brave knight on that instant softened his face and waves of his fiery eyes came together. She took advantage of the spiritual softness of the man and said:
- Brave man! - You know that Ela has been looking to confront you awhile ago. She made a mistake in trying to see your face without asking you first, but pardon her, please! The girl did not want to hurt you. She could not stop herself, because she was anxious with her desire to see your bright eyes. Then the chief braveman with his grey hair dropped the leash on the shoulder of the worried horse, grabbed his sword with the two hands, pointed it towards the people that were cheering "Long live the braveman" and slowly went to the body of Ela that was laying down, without consciousness. After bowing over her, he looked at his manlike fingers and when he wanted to extend his hand and to keep away her black hair that was covering her grim cheeks, she opened her eye lids. The man turned quickly his back towards the pretty lady, and, without saying a word, inserted his sword in the steel cover tied closely to his belt, then he was disappointed for not enjoying his beauty, he ordered his knights to hold the girl and place her again in her horse that was sitting nearby. The lady cook was quiet for a moment, but silence did not last for long. She was shaking now, was pushing with her elbows the energetic men that

were keeping her in the air. She did not want to give up without letting him know that she knew that person, but the attempt to get closer to him was totaly futile. The efforts to step away and her calls fell on deaf ears and were not doing anything. The knight had another longing. Now, when she felt dry like darkness and quiet like a rock, the powerful anger errupted inside the body with a wounded soul and her broken voice was cracked like a thunder:

-Hey you! You cannot close my mouth, oh chieftain of the two worlds! And if I hurt you for calling you as such, then I will call you as you prefer, but I cannot act as someone who does not know you. Yes, yes, I know you, knight. Why do you hide your face from me? As a little girl I have seen you everywere. I saw you very often in the room of men, hanging in the wall. And one day when my father was talking something quiet with your photo, I asked him who was this person with whom he was speaking so often?

- "Is the National Hero," – he responded while sitting with his crossed legs. But, at that time I was not understanding it. I was so little. In the painting I was only looking the frame of a man with a sharp face, big nose, and extended beard, that was not saying anything to me. My daddy who knew your importance, died with the longing that he could not go at your grave, beyond the border. Myself, as a poor orphan, decided to hang nearby your portrait the photo of my father. Now you both were together. And the little girl of a man that appreciated you until his death, every evening he went alone in his room and praying for you and himself. Yes, yes! I was kissing the sword of my dad, the front in the paper behind the glass. When I was older, but I could not touch it, I had no courage, they were not allowing me. I looked that they wanted you more than us, therefore they defend your sword in their own museums.

Perhaps we ignored you and for this we lost the right to keep your most precious belonging. Do you know how upset I was? I almost lost my mind! But I was sure that you loved so much your people, this is why you never let them down. So, please, do not hide your eyes, oh brave knight of my country. The Brave Knight, silently, had taken an unbreakable stature, and she, disappointed, was unstoppable, was speaking until running out of her voice:

-You, dear people, make sure to listen! I have met this knight many times in the class of history. There I learned that the sword of this man ... hey, you do not believe this? Yes, yes, of this man over here, changed not only the history of the Balkans, but also that of Europe. Turned towards him and said: - I entered in the Dead World only to meet with you, do you understand? I want to see your eyes so bad, because with your great stature I fell in love forever when I saw you in the Balkan's youngest capital city, sitting on top of the horse that is near you. Please, knight, do not hide your face because it hurts me. The prayers of Ela were shaking the earth below his feet. The man with his rising eyebrows could not resist to the words anymore. Suddently, he came around and fell into his knees before her. Everyone was surprised. The move of this great man made them silent. It had never happened before that a famous knigh would bend his knees before someone else. His attitude changed the spirit of the girl. Now they were equals. They both were sitting with their heads down before one another. For an instant the silhoutte of this great man was covering the body of Ela and with his long-extended hands he said to her:

-Come up girl of my family tribe.

Without even raising her head she said:

-I bow to you, - Oh knight. Tightly holding hands, they were deeply looking through the eyes of one another. Under the cheering of people "one living and a dead one became real friends". The brave man saw the eyes with tears of a vivid woman hero. Just like himself she was also confident that they loved each other. Glamorous calls of the people seemed to her as a refrain songs that make you fall asleep. Now the girl was dying for some sleep. She was looking for a place were to lay down. Her body was slipping slowly through the hands of this great man. The knight was worried that by showing his face something bad would happen, but not this one, not falling asleep. If he let her fall asleep, she would not wake up for seven hundred years. Then such a weakness would catch the other ones, because his objective was to put in deep sleep those people, this way he could steal their time, and invisibly he would take their freedom. Evil was acting in such a way so that everything could appear as nothing was happening.

-He is playing a bitter game, - started the chieftain. Then he made a ruthless front, raised his eyebrows and started to move Ela, who wanted to sleep unlike anyother time.

-Come up, please, because our people have slept more than earth in their own land. Is it enough five hundred years of winter and one hundred years of snow? Wake up, I beg you! – He was talking to the girl that succumbed into sleep and was not hearing anything.

-No, do not go, - he said while looking at Tana, that was approaching the uncontrolled feet of Ela. -Do not worry, we will not loose her. Go away. Leave us alone, - Tana responded.

The chieftain pulled himself on the side and was looking at them. He was afraid that the effort to wake up Ela could be tragic because he could even kill her, but, the rare moves of the girl's eye brows, that was almost falling in deep sleep, showed that her eyes with a violet color were becoming functional. That color was ruining her sleep in the eye pupils that were rolling around. The successor of Demon failed. Crunched with his shoulders and feet was acting as longing and full of anger was looking at the park that was echoing joy and love. Was looking at Ela, the brave man, women dancing below the sounds of the crazy music of the Violinist, the kids that were running and playing with one another, old men relaxing and men cleaning up their weapons. He brought his horns on his knees and with the head of fractured ideas screamed:

-I am longing because no one lets me dance, - he spoke looking at Tana.

-Yes but, you cannot dance with your head down. Neither alone.

-But I am not alone, - evil responded.

-Do not take me into account. Eventhough we are two, we are still one because I am not dancing anymore with evils, - she said, and sat over the white stone enjoying the beautiful atmosphere that Ela brough in the world of after-death. However, sorrow begun to deem his happiness, when he thought that after a while half of the people would be killed, perhaps she maybe one of the dead. Touched, was making a comparison of the lady that loved life and shared with others, and the life of the one that entered in the dark world only one moment and it was enough to make herself suffer. "the closer we are among one another, the further away we are" – she said. The man with a white beard and the woman with black hair were going towards her, and Tana was in the middle of people's happiness and the noise of destructive soldiers. Fell in the ground and observed with the face encompassed by soil.

-Soldiers of dinosaurs are close by, my chieftain.

-What are you saying? They are quick. We must leave now.

-Do you have a map? – questioned the girl of living word.

-No, we have no maps nor plans, - he responded. – We are always oriented towards the source of light, but everytime being careful. We don't know what is hiding before and behind us, here in the middle of light and there full of darkness, from the source of cold and here from the source of warmth but going back there is none. This road we will follow even at this time. It is a heavy duty to rescue all these people from the golden walls without falling in the hands of bad ones. The greatest burden is held by us chieftains and women. Especially the young mothers, that have taken the side of bad knights. The three men and Ela that were standing up already, gathered their swords gifted by the Prince and were committed that they would be in service of peace until their lives are dissolved. Surprisingly, in the peaks of sharp swords that were magically shining were shaped eight numbers. The four numbers in the first two swords, that started from the sword's edge of the Braveman, were similar with the other four numbers that ended at the sword of Ela. All of the numbers were equal two by two, swiftly, created a triangle that left outside the lady cook from these three points. The men of dead world were surprised. While they did not know what this triangle was about, they could not read the meaning of numbers.

-Is the triangle of Bermuda? No, no, - said again. – This is not. When trying to read it, a powerful energy mixed with a strong light threw it in the ground.

-What is this? – the knights of the World of Hell questioned. With all energy they tried to keep their swords together so that Ela would learn the message of this formula.

-The explanation of these numbers would be possible only when I return in the life from where I have come from, - she responded while dropped in the ground. – if it is a triangle, we will suffer together with you. Then the numbers started to disappear slowly together with the pressure of energy. The swords remained in the hands of braveman that were committed to liberate hell, and the attractive sounds of violin had covered the whole space. The garden was decorated by people that were not stopping their joyful moments. Ela felt sorry that happiness would not continue for long.

-Time does not allow for any longer, - the Brave man reminded the woman with whom he had fallen in love.

-I know! But when are they going to celebrate again like today? – said to him. This question he did not want to answer, even his conversation did not stop.

-Obviously, we will have to deal with the bad fighting knights, but the most important thing is that most of our dead can be replaced with the men from enemy's army. Mothers or women that have their sons and daughters within the side of enemy will spread good lives among their loved ones. So, the army of the bad ones will be weaker, and we will become stronger.

-Please Chieftain? Come before the people and invite them to get ready, - said Tana with her head squeezed on the chest. He was looking at how the people used freedom. Felt sorry for disturbing their celebration; but was shy to take a risk. Immediately rised up his sword. Before asking the knights to depart he said to the women and mothers to remain side by side with the Braveman. They were told that kids must be the first ones in the row looking towards the light, and those behind them, need to remain between men and kids to support both rows. The last rows must be taken by those armed because the enemy will come from the rear. Ela was delighted with the greatness of her brave man. The chieftain had a little time left to spend with the lady of his tribe, because they were almost there. He hugged her rapidly and with his powerful arms brought her above the horse like a timid hummingbird and said:

-Let's go. That is how it happened. The long lines were leaving a deserted path. They entered slowly in the giant forest full of snow, which was separating the knights with the light coming from there. The closer they came towards the forest engulfed into a bad weather; Tana felt that something mysterious was hidden below the cracking cover of the rock. With great interest was walking nearby the rocks that were raised in the shape of evils. It appeared that evils were opening their mouths of blasphemy, were pulling out their tongue and smiling out loud with the poor kids that were even weak to stand on their feet from fear. Suddenly his eyes went towards the girl that was scared and came nearby Ela slowly and inserted his hand under the blue mantle. When the Lady Cook was hurriedly trying to help the little one with a jacket and with jeans, hitting the ground before her feet, someone stopped her. Surprised she looked at the little girl with white hair that had placed her hand inside the warm mantle and she had'nt noticed. Tana smiled within herself, and Ela while not stopping at her pocket, fixed the scarf of the boy around his neck and without disrupting her view from him she placed the little girl under her arms she had the image of a frozen angel. The little girl squeezed the waist of the lady and pulled the coat towards herself to cover her soft body that was shaking. After she became a little warm, she talked crying: -I am an orphan and you look like my mother. I miss my parents. She went even closer to her because she was afraid that the lady would be going away. Ela wanted to give her the entire love of humanity. But she could not do anything except for keeping her warm and to caress her hair covered by mud that was encrusted by frost. Ela was deeply saddened from the suffering eyes of all orphans that were looking for a heart.

Chapter 11

Throughout the gorge of the forest was passing the brutal cold wind. The archer was carefully looking the terrain and was not allowing anyone from deviating from the row. Ela together with the knights were helping the kids to go up the frightening rock, while pursuing Tana across the semi-dark road filled with ball drops of snow. Little-flakes not only made it difficult for the people to see through, but they were also erasing the tracks left behind by those that could not be seen. The girl with violet eyes with her head resting over the chest, hair filled with snow and her athletic body, was leading the long caravan without any fear. The black crows, that were flying over the people's heads and the colony of bats came out of the dense Albanian forest, they were not comfortable there.

She was waiting that immediately after the flying mammals something would happen. She was not surprised at all, when a creepy shadow up to infinity, appeared in front of the people covering up the largest parts of Albanian forests. From the cave was heard a frightening scream, that indeed extended the rocks' major cracks all the way up to Tana's feet. The long lines of people stopped. The unarmed women were looking at the kids getting cold, whom, overwhelmed by sadness begun to spread on different directions. Those women immediately spread themselves and enclosed the kids in the middle and stated that nothing bad would happen to them. Ela with a little kid on her hands came close to the girl that had stopped and was keeping her head down. The little girl wanted to know what that scream was about.

-Shshsht...do not say anything please, - said Tana, - I need silence here. Ela stopped, but those frightened people did not stop. Then she rises her hand asking them to remain calm. Immediately silence spread all over the valley. The interesting scream was repeated for the second time and the rocks moved out of their beds. The girl with her head sitting on her shoulder was not moving, she was only measuring something with her fingers in the air. The steam coming from the convoluted mountain gorges was saying to all that it was connected to something dangerous.

-Is demon, - she said to her. On that moment, the girl was not worried about anything else except victory. For a lady to kill the evil, would be something very difficult, as the time to fulfill the promise made to one-self and to others had come. The ultraviolet rays were brewing hatered inside her. This burning power he had gifted to the lady without remembering that the moment would come when she would use that force for destroying his kingdom. In her body there was something that others did not have, this is why he wanted to have the war somewhere deep inside, because the kids had no guts to watch either him or the bad guys.

"If this happens, they will become older ahead of time," – was thinking the girl with a ruined long hair. Throughout her hair, that were dripping sweat and melted snow, she saw the poor kids, that had attached their faces over the chest of one – another and with their hands had closed their ears. Then with her ruined voice from frustration she called the bad guy: -Come out! Come out! I have no time to waist with you, you bastard! Come out! Come out I am talking to you as I am not scared of you. The purpose of Tana was so that she could make the Demon upset and pull him out as soon as possible in a dual fight. She did not want to involve five or six muscular fighters, that were running towards the cave to help her out. She wanted to quickly finish this fight because her companions would get killed for no reason.

-He was powerful, - Tana was thinking! – I am not afraid of Demon, those in service of evil must be afraid of those that light a wrong fire, - was screaming Tana. While looking at Ela, whose face was covered by tears, headed towards the rock and with the eyes that bothered her chest she disappeared in the abyss of the cave, right were the voice was coming from.

Chapter 12

Thunderstorm was not stopping. The Albanian Forest was shaking from within and the kids continued to keep their ears closed. Even the girl of living world had closed her eye lids and was moving only her lips. She was praying so that her friend would come out of the cave as victorious and in a good shape. As she was numbly waiting, someone squeezed her from behind. She knew her. It was Melani, whom she had not met since the time of being free from the Rock of Curse. The old lady had spent enough time with her family members and begged for pardon to the cook for leaving her alone. Everything was accepted in silence. Sitting next to one another, under the snowstorm, they were looking towards the entrance of the cave. Except for the wind breaking the silence, the breadth of people and walking routine of five or six knights that were dismantling the snow, nothing else could be heard. Everyone was focused in the rock and were waiting for Tana, who had entered inside the cave of screams while holding tight her sword.

The endless night made the girl to be careful while standing in the narrow corridors of Albanian mountains, the very same corridors that evil had built with a great mastery. The cave's tunnels were getting some light and wild shadows were following her up front and on the back. She was following them under the vague light of fire that was falling directly above the ugly corpses that were crawling amid those edges of rocks. She was already nearby the gate of the terrible evil; that was guarded by two frightening soldiers. They wished her a welcome and shifted the rock. The big stone was rolling, the gate was opened and the two were in front of each other. They were not talking, neither looking upon their faces. She pulled out her black coat to avoid any obstacles, rise her head up and full of energy remained in front of the Monster. Her violet eyes were controlling every movement through her long-unleashed hair dropped before her face. The wide shoulders of the chest had equipped the lady with an image of unwavering powerful man. She was holding the sword with great ease on the right hand, while with the other hand was feeling its sharp edges. Her breadth was growing ever more. Was walking carefully and making smart moves. Was looking at Monster – Demon that was sitting comfortably on his throne and was unworried about her. These tragic, cruel images surprised her. The body of the Monster, three times larger than her body, was sitting on top of the gold of entire world and was holding three scary heads with six elongated hands like hands of dragons that could not wait until breaking someone apart. The head in the middle was the saddest one, and the two heads on both sides were similar with the one in the middle, but with small differences. The two heads on the sides were a little smaller and quieter, they had no eyes and always were run by the head in the middle. In that face covered by bumps were hiding two red eyeballs, without any eye pupils, that were looking on all sides. She remembered that Evils have no eye pupils. They never look straight and don't look in the eye because they are liers, this is why with the passing of time they have earned the vision by looking on the sides. That is why, this vision particularity would have him killed today, because Tana before killing herself, evils took away her vision, this is why she had the same vision peculiarity as those evils.

And for this reason, she could hit her enemy without looking in his eye and when no one is expecting it. The girl was looking at the two twisted horns, but not so big, over the exposed front, the mouth was bloody naked, with those teeth out and the tongue like that of a snake that was coming around his neck, while being able to lick his elongated chin like the one of the old goat, meanwhile the thick tail was covering the most intimate parts of his body. The Demon had plenty of time, therefore he was not in a hurry.

He grabbed the cup filled with a coffee colored liquid and shook his gold looked like he wanted to find the end of it. Then he stood up and shameless for his naked body, started to laugh and requested even more drinks from his servants. They brought him other drinks, immediately. Proud for the bad things that he had been doing, was walking towards Tana amid the tall fire flakes everywere in the cave, which made his skin appear just like a rotten sea alga.

- "To hit him from here is far away", - was thinking Tana that was feeding her nerves for not loosing control before his energy.

-"I am not afraid of men! What about you lady, would you want to fight with me? He said and laughed while bringing out his teeth of sadness. Tana had no time to speak with him, but she was measuring the distance that told her "is still far away". Then she came closer slowly and when she was sure that distance was good enough to kill him, she screamed so loudly that it was heard from the people standing outside the cave.

-May you be burned in the flames that you have lit, oh Evil! She went straight to the Demon. Her opened eyes were throwing the force of ultraviolet rays, that were penetrating in her body. Even the circles of fire that were exhausted with the bad owner were gathered with the powerful rays of Tana and they ruthlessly burned the body of Demon. The Demon was becoming smaller and smaller before the brave girl that took him on surprise and was not stopping from destroying him. He was not expecting this end. When Demon noticed that he was almost finished, fell into his knees and with his nails was scraping the soil. Then he put up his crooked hands towards the girl, with his lips full of saliva asking for piety:

-I beg you to please! Pardon me! Pardon me, please! I know that I have caused you so much harm. Give me a chance to be better, - he said and crumbled fell on the ground.

-The ones that are killed may not pardon you, - responded Tana. – No, my eyes cannot pardon you. Here, look what you have done to them. And with the sword held tight she cut his bigger head. And the other two heads fell in the ground, but the breadth of suffering that came from his heads blew the girl strongly towards the nearby rock. The Demon died and the girl layed at the stone before closing her eyes forever, was looking again at the body of Demon that was burning in fire and her eyes slowly and at peace were pouring unique rays. Happy for destroying the spiritual killer of people she departed from life to land in peace. At that moment, the Albanian forests embodied a great echo. Everyone backed off, and the fighters that were running towards Tana, stopped. Shocked they looked towards the forest that was thundering and appearing like a soil full of volcanoes. The fiery stone pieces were pouring everywhere through the snow and were dissolving before the soldiers' feet. Everyone saddened bowed their heads. Everything with the Demon ended, but they lost their best fighter, and Ela lost her beloved friend. Her tears were crawling below her skiny cheeks. In those painful moments she observed the white dust in the figure of Tana that was rising and then was steadily spreading in space. She knew that the girl with her ruined hair could not be accompanied with her again, perhaps only in a dream. She was covered by sorrow even more when she realized that she would never know, were and in which place would be gathered the particles of Tana's beautiful soul.

Chapter 13

The cloud of dust that had covered the sky of hell was clearing quickly, but the silence of pain was still dominant. It was heard only the noise of the chieftain's boots as they were cutting the frozen snow heading towards Ela that was staying in silence. Her heart recognized his steps. She was shaking. She felt the proximity of the man with red mantle. He was already staying very close and was anxious to hug, squeeze her, but he was not doing it due to respect for the crying eyes. Ela engulfed by sadness had caught the fingers of the little girl and was letting them go. Saddened she was trying to hide her tears that were rolling above her cold cheeks. The brave man was losing his patience. Opened his arms and layed the woman on his chest. Suddenly he felt something that was moving through the body covered by stones. Warmth of the lady cook was penetrating inside the veins of the Knight. Ela attached to the man's body, forgot with whom she was dealing with. At the moment when his heart was beating strongly in her chest, she raised her head and saw him in the eyes. She wanted to stop her tears at this moment, was fighting with them, although they did not ask her. Tears had exploded and were continuing with their path. Then the girl renounced the chrystal liquid, revealed the palm of her hand, kept it tightly in the entrance of the cage and was listening his soft breadth. The Braveman was breathing with the same rhythm of her soul. Without detaching himself from the warm body, under the flocks of snow that were dripping through the rosy red faces, was feeling the pulses of a man's heart, a man that was very strong, wild and proud. In these moments attached to the body of one another she said: "We lost one life and we won another one."

The little girl had kidnapped Ela's hand and purposely remained in the middle of her hands. The kid did not want to abandon the body of Ela and was not even thinking to leave. She wanted Ela for herself and started to hate the Braveman, that was keeping her in his chest. The Knight, brave man did not see the kid, this is why he was sqeezing Ela even more. The tear of the woman that exploded was burdening the man further, but he felt that over there was starting something new, something pretty that gave a meaning to life. Inside his body exploded the fire of love that was not stopping him. With plenty of lust he touched her lips. The kiss made miracles. A divine brightness entered in the middle of them. Their hearts exchanged their places. Everyone around was mesmerized, meanwhile the two of them continued to kiss eachother without noticing that time was going. Melani, that was observing everything from nearby went slowly at the girl with silver hair and begged her to step away from them for just a little time, to leave them alone. The nervous girl was pushing the old lady to enter inside and got even more inside under the blue mantle of the lady cook. The old lady became upset.

- "How can Ela dare to play with time? Every second is priceless. Delay will bring everything backwards. Then the road to the Tower of Peace was long. I must distract them right away," – was talking the old lady and while shaking her two hand palms she noticed that her hands were red. "Hand clapping could bring them back to shape," - she said with her voice. "Yes, yes, it is a marvelous idea," so without loosing anytime she started to clap her hands.

With her face smiling she invited the other ones to do the same thing. From the claps of the dead people the Albanian forest was blowing up. They were surprised. They did not conceptualize what was going on. Shameful they saw one another and separated themselves. Melani was smiling with her face turned towards the little girl who blinked her eye to the old lady. The Braveman saw Ela with her yellow hair, nervously raised his eyebrows and right there started the fierce rivalry among them. The Braveman and the little girl wanted Ela only for themselves. As they were ready to fight, the Holy Spirit fell upon the crumbled rocks and quickly headed towards Ela: -Hurry up! The knight of bad ones has separated the army into two groups. He ordered one group to be in your pursuit. His purpose is to divide and destroy all of you from inside, because many of the fighters are those men and women coming from the city were they have a blood Feud...and when you will be weaker from fighting one another, they will prevail over you. The other half of the army was sent to the city of women. He will arive before you do. I am afraid from the Mother of Peace. She had only a few people to fight over there, - she said and disappeared in the dust that was flowing in space. The eyes of women in the dead world were wide open. They would be fighting after a while. They started to cry and with their two hands they squeezed their cheecks while saying: - Oh God! We must fight against our kids. Let them kill us or we kill them? Oh God, where are you? Ela, while she had taken some courage now from Tana and wanted to bring some energy from the power of God that was sleeping, raised her head and spoke like a prophet.

-Do you want to return again to your kids? The women stopped the slaughter.

-You mothers, will not fight just like I did in not fighting anyone. You will give your own lives to men and girls for the second time. So, you will fight with the power of love to have born babies in all your hands. Please, remain calm and wait for the right moment. They were in front of her and waiting for the instant of pains. -We should fight and even must be the first ones in the frontline, -there came a rebellious voice from the crowd of ladies that confused everyone. The lady with her ruined hair under her white head cotton cover, that the wind was moving sometimes before and then behind her shoulders, was walking towards Ela.

She was equally decent and gigantic at the same time. She had placed her right hand on the left side of the chest and with her opened hand palm was caressing the life. - Where is this lady coming from, with this interesting costume? – Melani was asking Ela. The lady cook was squeezing her shoulders. Was looking at the old cloth towel that the brave lady had placed on her head while leaving totally open her face and neck. The white blanket covering her hair represented the genuineness of a determined lady, conservative and fully conscious for her actions. The dark mantle covered by flowers, was covered little by little from a thin cover of snow, but the white flakes could not cover the red petals. They were not deemed yet by soil. The two frontal angles of this handkerchief had fallen over the agrandized chest of the girl and were touching her silver decorations. The lady cook was convinced that the hand that had made this dress was gifting endless love. Marveled from this dress she saw her from head to toes. She observed the grey shirt, that must have been white at some point, was like a long traditional wide skirt of night until the knees. This skirt was tied strongly around the waist by two whool cords. The back part was covering only her back side and her body could be seen only when the wind would be moving that cover piece, and the tallest one was tied as a cooking apron that was coming around her waist and waved down, hitting her knees. At the corner of the rope costume was knitted a sun with a light brown color. The straight and thick feet of the girl were covered by the black socks. Everything was knitted by hand and with the same cotton fabric and sewing fibers. She was looking at the shoes made out of bull's skin to avoid any concern coming from old women around. The latest dress was a mantle that Ela liked it very much over all other dresses. The mantle that remained inflated, had an interesting shape. Was decorated around with whool made instruments and different religious symbols: such as the cross, bell, then the sun, moon, the proud head of a bull, all combined professionally.

The wool mantle with his sleeves that could not be worn, but that remained hanging on both sides of the chest, was covering the clothes worn in the body of the lady. - "What is this? What is the name?" – was thinking the lady cook that was looking her with envy. She was silenced a little and said: - "Oh! Yes. This is called "*Gunë*. Yes, yes, this is *Gunë*."[2] She remembered when going with her father in the museum and the guide was explaining to visitors the work done by her. The man was explaining that it was elaborated with a wool, this is why people were using it in wintertime. Not only it is very pretty and warm it is also somewhat heavy to carry. This old, ancient dress has been and is still worn by an ancient and brave nation that still is living there, when God created this earth and named it Balkan. "Oh, I love so much this dress, but I must have a body for it." Ela was looking with envy how the shoulder cover was flowing on the body of the blessed lady. The lady that was holding Guna was not focused at all on how hard it was to keep it or about its look as a piece of wool, but she was worried for the poor kids. The midget lady was not breathing well from the pain she felt for them. She looked at them how fragile and defenseless they were; therefore, she was committed to dedicate her life to kids. She swallowed her saliva once and said: -I became a bride, but never a lady nor a mother. This is why I promise that from today my heart is beating for the orphans of the poor world. The words that came from her mouth on those moments made her the Queen of Besa[3]. Ela admired the lady

---

[2] Gunë: a thick clothing, made of goat's wool like a long cape gown to the knees, sleeveless and with a hood, which shepherds usually wear to protect themselves from the cold and rain. A shepherd's Guna. Once August and summer are over, clothes lina Gunë and food are needed to keep you warm.

[3] Besa is an Albanian cultural precept, usually translated as "faith", that means "to keep the promise" and "word of honor". The only word in

with that beautiful Gunë. Her front was opening for the girl of her earth, meanwhile the Chieftain was delighted by her. He was already listening to other ladies that were covering the voice of silence and commitment that their lives did not belong only to their kids by blood, but to all orphans that would cover every corner of the valley.

- "The heart of the lady invades the world, but the heart of mom also invades God," – said the Braveman to himself and jumped over his horse and pursued the end of his caravan.

Shqip (language of the Eagle) that can be translated as 'faithful' is 'besnik', derived from besa. Besnik for masculine and Besa for feminine continue to be very popular names among the people of Shqiperia (land of the Eagle). Some say that the word 'besa' traces back to the Kanun of Lek Dukagjini, a collection of laws which regulated the Albanian social, economic and religious lives, together with traditional customs and cultural practices of the Albanian society since the XV century until today. Besa is an important part of personal and familial standing and is often used as an example of "Albanianism". 'Besa' has been an integral part of the Shqiptar (people of the Eagle), since ancient times. It represents unity among the different indigenous tribes of that land. The unity of 'besa' (a moral code that was deemed higher in value than any other imposed religious beliefs on that land) made it possible for the Shqiptar to survive the various forms of ethnic cleansing from various foreign invasions and hostile neighbours.

Chapter 14

The blue color was confining quickly the broken Albanian Forest that was willing to handle the foot paths of good soldiers. Now everything was breathing freely. The Queen of Besa was releasing their heavy steps to a point that their feet were burning. She was walking over the stones with the feeling that she would squash again the heads of evils and breaking their horns. The last object she stepped on was a part of Demon's arm that was burned by fire. Time after time the lady was turning her head while looking at the people that were following her. She was even looking at the kids that were still scared and kneeling their body when they were passing in front of the frightening figures. They all together were walking towards the origin of light, and, when the first lady passed the ruins, the bride opened her eyes in the horizon. In front of her appeared the blue sky that surprised her. The leveled rock and the dead sea were not impressed. The Sea was motionless, without any sand, without any waves and ships, without any fish nor whales. There were not even any mammals with the exception of some wooden skeletons that had survived. She did not feel good, but the blue light was expanding even more making her peaceful and gave her strength to come near the shore.

-Isn't there perhaps the Golden Tower? – she thought. – Isn't it true for bad knights to have passed in here? No, I don't think so! There are no traces that someone has been here before us. It is impossible, - said the Queen of Besa and her face got bitter from fear that they may not reach other side of the shore.

- Here is possible to go through? What? From where? To cross this sea is equally impossible with the inevitable fact that we are unable to bring back all people from the dead world into the living world.

-Are these rivers the two branches in front of us? – asked! Saddly she moved her head on the right and then on the left, afterwards moved again on the right and her eyes cought something that she could not identify clearly. Her medium size height made her stand on top of her fingers and to extend her neck on the right side. "This is so bad," - she whispered and with her index finger was drawing in space. The point of her finger from far away was touching something in the shape of a triangle. But what is this? She tried to remember, but she could not remember as to what kind of object was similar to that black object? It had gone away from her memory or she may have never known. Then she placed her hand on the top front. Even though she felt annoyed to ask the girl of living world, she said: -What is that surprising object? Ela analyzed it and said: -This is called a pyramid, - she responded and remembered her math class that she did not enjoy at all. It was monotonous and hard for her. When the teacher was asking her students, about the total amount of angles in one triangle, she was looking outside the window, because she was interested on this subject. The girl was eager to participate in the history class. Fortyfive minutes were too short for her. She either loved this class or liked the charismatic teacher, the way he was explaining his lessons, and made students to remember the lecture content for a long time.

The pyramid that was overlooking from far away, at these moments reminded her the lecture about Egypt. She had carefully followed the teacher as he had told them that in Egypt there are many pyramids. He had explained to them that they were solid and built by slaves, whose main ethnicity was Hebrew. According to biblical recording, he said: hebrews were the selected people of God. Perhaps this is why they are very smart, because those objects would not be existing for millions of years without getting ruined and in their inner walls would be buried pharaohs and kings of those old times.

- Don't you think, this is the tower that we defend? – said the Queen of Besa and silently she headed towards the sea with her two opened arms. Her left arm was dead, and the other one extended towards the right of the girl. In her twisted shoulders was shaped a giant river with a sweet water and with wonderful layers of ice. The midget girl immediately came close to the edge of solid water and was measuring with her eyes the icy parts, that wild time had crafted them with great mastery. Under the transparent chrystal was looking at the water, that was pouring silently while not bothering the other crazy part of sea. Was looking at large and small stones, white and black, round and sharp stones so sharp, as their peaks had cought the ice and had come out above the dough surface, while causing hell with a good environment. Impressed with the beauty that was looking she said:

-Oh yes not the entire hell is a disaster. There are even better and beautiful things. Confused because she was not further closed in the rocks of evil and had withheld her life on her hands she did not feel at all the kid with red hair that was pulling her towards the Guna of whool until he started to call her:

-Hey, hey...

-What do you want?

-What is your name, -he asked.

-Nora, - she responded.

-They are coming, - said the boy while shaking and grabbed the scarf even closer to his weak neck.

-And you, why are you afraid? – said the Queen of Besa, and the taste for pretty ice was dissolved. She saw the river which appeared to go crazy and wanted to kidnap the kids. Opened the eyes around and observed a rock sitting nearby.

-The house is the only possibility to defend them, - she thought and immediately left after the orphans, who were all confused from panic. Their majority were not able to take care of themselves. They were blind, without any feet, and without any hands or only with a foot and the other one was artificial, "a Foot" which the parents had thrown in the grave on the day of funeral, because they believed that it could be useful to the kid even on the other world. Other parts of the body they kept with great care because they were happy to have saved them from the bombs of crazy times.

Ela with her red eyes was looking with a great admiration towards Nora whose nick name was also a midget girl. She was running like thunder and left no child outside except the one with curly hair, which was so tight with her body. After placing all of them in the dark room she spoke with the lady cook:

-Both of you can come inside. Get inside and please do not come out until one of us would be calling you. The lady of living world could not do any more except to find a shelter, but before getting inside, she gave her the sword, because while knowing how to use those weapons, she would be fighting relentlessly. Subsequently by handing her the sword she said:

-This is for you. Please take it, because I am afraid of the sword. After a while silently entered in the cave, opened the arms as much as she could and held tight the orphan over the warm chest. Then the short girl closed the entrance with a big stone, erased the flip flopes and with two heavy swords she disappeared. The little girl with a snow like hair was so close to Ela that she could not breath comfortably. Lips that were shaking were looking for something. The girl had befriended someone.

-Where is Melani? Hey were is she? – she talked with a quiet voice, pulled her head from the brest of the lady cook and begun to cry and only cry.

Suddenly someone came behind her shoulder and caressed her well shaped long hair. The little girl with frozen hair turned her head towards the warm hand. After she saw her, left the chest of Ela, and escaped in the chest of her grandmother that was waiting for her with open arms.

Chapter 15

The Queen of Besa like a powerful wind, returned to her people. Was looking painfully the grim faces of those moms. Women had lost the brightness of their eyes. They knew that war in order to sit the kids again in their warm lap, it was even more painful than the day when they were born. But, decision for return of loved ones was not equal even with the precious life and for them giving their lives it meant to be reborn. With all of the danger, those moms requested to be the first ones in the frontline. They were sitting in a row as they pleased. Like silent and devoted women soldiers they remained up front. The long rows were waiting for Nora to give the order. In these moments, the Midget Girl noticed that they felt lost. To say it directly to those moms that destiny of those kids today was depending on them, was very hard for her. She did not want to burden them even more. Then she bowed a little and spoke further:

-My dear women! We are infront of a war full of pain, but today we will fight with the power of love. This type of war no one can break. I am confident that we will get our reward. Please be very careful on whom you will kill. If you are hit without giving your life you are killed twice. Those killed twice cannot revive again their life and started to go through the rows in order to discuss with the Chieftain, who was somewhere by the end. Everyone was opening the path for him. She was walking like a real Queen, while looking at those moms that had their sons and daughters on the side of enemy, then she observed the good knights. In the last rows were staying the older ones. In the atmosphere of war, they appeared to be happy and unwavering. They were optimists that they would come victorious from their fight with those bad Knights.

Now everyone was waiting for Nora and the Brave man, they were talking together and pointing out with their hand towards those areas were dust was rising. She was saying to him something when she noticed that someone was coming closer. She pulled immediately her sword and wanted to hit the woman that she didn't know.

-Don't kill me, - she said! Wasn't you the lady who said that who is killed for the second time cannot be reborn again? I want to live! If you allow me, I want to serve all of you, moms, orphans, because I am also a mother, I have also left my kids as orphans. I didn't want to leave them alone in such early stage, because they are still young, and through the tears that covered the green eyes she said: - They sent me here without my wish. They were obstructed by the echo of my voice, expressed on paper.

My writing, were not only bothersome but also were dangerous for them, this is why they sent me here, were at least I wanted to come, was talking the lady with her hair still clean and organized, with clothes sprinkled with mud, well polished shoes and a thick bag hanging between the arms and neck, from which she pulled a notebook with white papers, folded neatly. When the young lady was carefully reviewing the thin pages, the Queen of Besa came close and saw the empty page of the notebook that was filling up with little writing.

-What is this? What are you drawing? – Nora asked her.

-I am not drawing, - I am writing. I am taking notes, - she responded with great warmth and sweetness so the snowflakes were dissolving before they would fall on the pages of the notebook.

-I am a journalist. I have come in your world to take an interview with the dead people, - she said with great humor and started to smile. – Hey, you see? We are so energetic as even when we are dead we still work hard, she laughed. Everyone was looking at her with a great surprise on what she was talking and started to talk to one another. Many of them did not know the meaning of the word journalist, even the Midget Girl who enjoyed those letters, had no idea.

-Over there are not interested with those looking after the light, - she started to talk. – If you aim, aspire light, - they burn your life. As she said these words, she lost her desire to make jokes. She was a little shocked and with her sad face, she placed her notebook on her bag and when she opened her new vest to place her pen in the pocket of white shirt, some drops of blood dripped below her chest. Nora understood that another woman had just disappeared from the dark world and had come into the world of hell. She admired the courage of that lady, who she had to call as a journalist. She wanted to take her with herself, and without saying a word she placed the sword into her. She did not refuse it. She took it in her hands and saw the lower part of its edges. Was the sword of Tana that the lady cook had discovered below the crumbled rocks. The lady of writings saw Nora, then the sword, and said: -Thank you my dear! My weapon is the pencil. Nora understood the lady of the pencil, took the sharp sword from her hand, inserted it in the waist and went together with those women, that were waiting orders from her, while not hiding their fear.

Chapter 16

The earth had started to vibrate. The heads of bad people had surpassed the space. They did rise their weapons in the air and with the noise of monsters did not allow the good people to be at peace. Even the Braveman was worried. He was worried that he would be losing a lot of people and would lose his war. Standing on top of the horse was moving up and down. Was not staying in one place. The sword of steel he didn't pull out of his waist. With one hand he kept the horse's leash, and with the other was caressing his beard that was intertwined with the rising hair of the horse. Half of his hair like snow was flying in space and other half were falling over his shoulders, while covering the sharp arms of the eagle that were fierce and ready to defend the Head of Braveman who was never tired from holding the eagle over his wide shoulder. The fiery eyeballs of the Chieftain invaded the territory and afterwards they stood in front of those moms and expressed their appreciation by looking at them. He saw Nora and the journalist, then he said:

-I don't have enough time, because we are now in front of a fight and that will not be the last one. So please, take good care of your loved ones and those of you that have swords must hit only the enemy, because for the bad ones will be a loss if they are overthrown by women that happen to be the soul of this world. When he mentioned the women, he took silence. At that moment he was missing someone. Something was missing, and, in the absence of someone, he felt his chest while listening the speeding rhythm of that half, of that vital thing. Addicted from his chest beats, he talked again: Let no one try to take what belongs to us. We will never allow it.

The sharp edges of the man's sword were shining towards the army of Rhyno, that was approaching fastly with the steps of evil. In the moment of departure, the Queen of Besa went in front of the man's path. Wait! Today women will attack first. We think this is better.

-Please! – she said to him. He did not say a word. He only saw them being impressed and stepped aside.

Chapter 17

Over the territory that was covered by thunders of war appeared again the Holy Soul. The bird with the shape of man, was staying in the air and looking at the two parties. Was looking at the eyes full of light amid the great fighters that were eager for the war to start and come victorious at the end. Was looking at the dark eyes and full of hatred by steel fighters that were looking only for blood. The bird was looking at the deemed faces and mouth of the two Chieftains, that would be opened from one instant to the next to initiate the skirmishes of a bloody war.

The man dressed in steel from his head to toes was staying in the middle of battlefield with his long fighting arrow in front of his soldiers. His disoriented eyes were looking for his counterpart in the middle of hundreds and thousands of women that were ranked in the field. He was afraid of light, men, presence, and charm of women fighters. Above all the enemy was saddened from those women's silence. He was moving his head nervously from one side to the other, so that the bones in his neck and his rotten jaws were cracking. Women! But who are these? What do they want over here? – Frightened from what was happening, he questioned: - where are the men? Where is the Brave Man? He started to call him with a loud voice. –Where are you? Why are you hiding behind the women? Are you a coward man, or what? Why are you doing this? Hey, why are you hiding behind these disabled women? He was screaming and laughing with irony, in order to advance the moral on himself and his soldiers, that were having a good time after what their Chief had just said, covered from head to toe with a black uniform.

The word "useless" made the women really upset. This pressured them to not take orders from anyone, but to head towards him with the advise of the Braveman that "your sword would not miss the target" and with the voice of Nora "caution and avoid getting killed and careful on who you kill". The fight started. The good and the bad were placed in front of each other. The swords of moms were rising with all the energy and hit the bones of those ugly evil men. Meanwhile Nora without any fear, aimed at the charcoal face of the enemy's Chieftain that was becoming crooked. With the rising sword and the voice of war she run towards him as the son of evil was staying next to him and saying "You are scared for sure? She is a woman. You do not need to fight. With women one can only play."

-If I don't fight with her, she may kill me, are you stupid! – he responded to the evil's son and immediately their swords were crossed in the air, not with Nora, - but with the sword of Braveman.

-The evil in miniature, remained in the middle of three flames, and then crolling around he immediately left.

-"Evils are lucky", - he said to himself and was hiding behind a rock formation that was nearby, and the Queen of Besa pulled immediately after she heard the Chieftain with the red mantle saying: "My love! Leave it no me." Saddened that she did not have the delight to kill the bad guy by herself, she carefully stepped aside leaving the two men fighting with each - other. Concentrated at her instinct that the commander of enemy had prepared a secret strategy, it was not a lie. With attention she was looking at many enemy fighters, that were attacking with a great impact, they were not equally armed. "Those that are on the attack are better prepared," – she thought in herself the Queen of Besa. There has never happened before, in her fighting experience, something like this magnitude. Focused in the ruthless stage of war she was looking at the youngsters, with their numb hands and disoriented had no idea were to attack, how to defend themselves and were missing knowledge on how to attack.

What if they stayed?

Where?

And if they left, were?

Who to kill and who to save?

The men throwing a barrage of arrows towards Nora's people, convinced and pressured Nora to keep in the middle the arrowman of the attacker's army. The body of the poor archer fell in the ground like a dried wood log. The only thing that was left from him were the steel armor, sword and arch with arrows damped in the nasty soil moist, that now were taken by a young fighter with wide shoulders. He was totally lost and without thinking any second, he pointed out the weapon towards the woman who saw him in his eye and mentioned his name. But the sharp wood that took aim to the lady, was faster than her voice. The arrow hit straight the heart of fighters. The young boy opened his eyes while slowly talking:

-Oh God! – he recognized the voice. He recognized the scream. Was his mother that had fallen in the ground. Saddened he came close by, fell in his knees, he grabbed her quickly and placed her in his icy chest. She, before closing her eyes, saw the face of her soul, descended her hand over the heart's chest of her son and was giving him life for a second time. The blood veins of the young boy were filling with blood. The dark skin was becoming red and while accepting the rebirth, sometimes he was looking at his bloody hands and sometimes looking at his mother and his tears were falling over her face that was slowly laying down. The young man was talking to her, was begging a pardon, was saying that he loved her and was pleasing her to not depart from life, but now everything was too late. His mother was losing all energy, her voice was diminishing, her eyes were dying slowly, and her ruined heart was over. His mother is gone.

-How stupid was I, - he said giving the impression that he was at peace! – How stupid I am, - He said again and then with all his drive he screamed again: how stupid I was! How was I not able to understand how much she had loved me. I did not deserve this great mother.

After the huge mistake that he had committed, deep sorrow was pulling him in the abyss. Was exhausted even with the conscience of a reborn person, he sat on his crossed feet in the middle of a massacre, with full of life and empty hands. His eye lids were closing in the dust that was covering his dry lips. His ears were echoing bad, he could not even stand up. He fell and with his hands he hugged someone that was not with him anymore.

Chapter 18

The two sides were fighting for life. The stone hearted ones were fighting to eliminate life, the good ones were eager to defend it, while the son of Evil that was fanning the fire of war, was hiding behind the rock with a few people and were looking what was happening. In regard to their entertainment they started a betting game. Evil had much wealth, but why would not he take even the sweat of the stupid ones! With all his pleasure to see the invading army win, he placed his bet on the favor of the good army.

-Dance brother as much as you want. You will come wet out of this, were saying his friends. Wealth is ours because you have lost this bet. Evil was smiling. He knew that the second, defender's army was going to win and continued dancing. He was happily licking his lips and was wiping his small horns, until the sharp weapon, shaped like a sickle, roving in the air almost cut his head. Like a lightening he entered behind the rock and confused he touched his horns to make sure that they were still in place. When he saw that everything was in place, he continued to play the game without looking towards the weapon, that flew across the space and entered in the middle of two girls. The sickle had touched a little, unarmed both girls and then hit the stone hard, making a few sparkles and fell at the feet of those women. The girl that was nearby Nora, was impressed. She did not notice her wound, but she saw the sharp edge that had touched the Midget Girl. She grabbed the steel on her hands and was surprised when she saw a few red drops through the half-circled edge.

-What is this? Blood?

-Yes, yes, blood, - Nora responded.

-You are alive, -she said surprised.

-Yes, I am alive and living, was responding the revitalized girl. She carefully raised her hand and touched her in the rotten wound.

Suddenly from her deep wound was starting to drip blood.

-Oh God! I am living! Hey, people, I am also living. I have a soul, flesh, and blood. Inside me there is life. She opened and closed her fist. While looking at the surface of her hand, she saw the veins that were turning red. She touched her face. Was screaming and jumping from happiness without even thinking that war was going on around her. At the end she stopped to give a hug to the Midget Girl. The Queen of Besa resting down on him was saying something on his ear. She was calm and was listening to the unknown lady. She was shaking her head up and down and went towards the young boy that was drawing, while Nora on that moment, asked her.

-What is your name?

-Melina, -she responded. Now her long grey hair was visible and covering her shoulder and the two fingers rising.

-Girl of Peace, - Nora named Melina on a bright morning and continued to fight, and she quickly treespassed the obstacles and arrived at the young boy. She sat down on her knees and said to him: -Stand up, please. Stand up, I said! There are no people without mistakes. You are not doing anything with this, - she said to him.

-I am the mistake of God, - he continued and was clapping his dusty hands to see on who was ordering him so sweetly.

-No you are not failed. God does not fail, - said the girl who had extended her hands towards the fighting boy that was not willing to move.

-In the name of your mother I say to you: Stand up! For her sake, stand up! She loved you so much and for everything bad you had brought to her life; her soul has never cursed you. So please don't hurt your mother any further. Stand up! Make her happy! His eyes fell peacefully in the red face of the girl with curly hair. Impressed from the women's beauty, he stood up, opened his arms and exploded into tears before her.

-You are pretty very pretty to be loved, -he said to her! –Not for war, not to die. Attached to her shoulders, he wanted to grab her weapon.

-No, -responded the Girl of Peace without detaching herself from his body. – I need this one. You have one and if you want two, then you must find it yourself. With their bodies tied, they looked at the eyes of one another. When the young boy pulled his body a little so that he could see her lips turned red like blood, beyond her chest noticed the soldier covered with steel raising his sword to hit the pretty Girl of Peace.

-You even want to take this from me? – he screamed like crazy and jumped over the fighting warrior who wanted to kill the girl. Their clash lasted only a few seconds and the sword of the bad soldier was found in the hand of the young boy with a white wool albanian hat. The young couple hugged each other so tightly and took a deep breath, at a point that there was no room for air. In the flame of war the young boy continued to have his lips warm like charcoal. He could not resist. He kissed the girl so passionately and said: - You are filling the second half of my soul. You are everything that I have now and everything that will keep me in my life, my dear. "From today on I will live for the one that just left me and for the one that just came to me", he was thinking within himself. The girl could not see the young boy. She felt ashamed. She wanted to escape. She took a peek towards the nearby battlefield. She thought that they had gone a little far from the valley of clashes. She felt bad. Her companions needed her and meanwhile she was kissing. Then she started to shake up the young fighter next to her, who wanted to continue and stay like that.

-Hey, I am going, - she said to him and like a lightening the Young Girl went to help the grey woman, that was pulling with one hand the wounded girl and with the other hand was fighting against the enemy soldier, a cruel fighter that was hitting the women really hard in order to get them both killed, mom and daughter.

The Young Boy remained with his opened mouth our of surprise! How brave were the two ladies, up to the point when the sword of the bad soldier cut the hair from the woman's daughter. His eyes were burning. He became endlessly bitter. He grabbed the arch and without any mercy he hit with an arrow the enemy's ruthless fighter right in the middle of his throat. The Soldier's body covered by steel made a nasty voice and fell in the ground. The mother had no time to express her gratitude. The woman was fighting with her daughter that was heavily wounded and was refusing to live. The mom had opened the hand of her daughter and was listening to her heart that was not beating. Was calling her name. Was begging, but it was pointless. She was not responding. Then she made a fist out of her hands and while hitting her chest with all she had in her chest, and she said:

-I am, your mother, I order you: Wake up! Unfortunately even this tactic was not working. She gave up. She dropped her head over her daughter's dead body and succumbed into tears. Suddenly someone touched her well knitted long hair. The lady did not move. She would not believe that her daughter was alive again. Incredibly happy she could not escape from her chest.

- Thank you, mom!
- Shshsh...don't talk! What I did, is so little. Life has just started, my dear. And right there nearby, was listening to her heart beats, and for the little musician was enough a brief look to see his mother and sister going towards him. Hope that they would be together one day, never faded away in him. Even though he had waited for a long time to meet with them, he did not open his arms to hug them, but he grabbed his violin, stood on top of a rock and was playing the instrument with great energy in order to give more stamina to the Brave Fighter, whose sword was hanging now over the head of the enemy forces' commander and the Fighter's eyes were sprouting fire.
- Take away that steel mask from your head and do not make any stupid move, - he said to him! Otherwise you are dead. The grey eyes were confronted with the golden eyes of the Brave Fighter, who had placed his foot over his shoulder and was impulsive from the hate that he had harbored for him. The Leader with a double headed eagle was not willing to see the enemy's face anymore.
- Cover up your face, ugly looser, - he said. – Take the horse and get out of here! Go and tell your Chieftain how bad it was for all in this battlefield and that everyone will end like you. The Commander of enemy forces, who was selling bravely minutes ago, placed his hat above his head, started to run, jumped over the stallion, and left behind his dead soldiers. Covered by fear, looked at Evil behind the rock counting his money earned from the recent betting. With a deep disappointment that Evil had abandoned him, he hit the shoulders of his horse and left the battle scene.

Chapter 19

The war had torn apart the strength and power of people, that were taking a break in the wider battlefield. The young ladies were treating the wounded. The journalist was asking some of them and wrote in the white paper. Many knights rested over the grass were responding to her and were looking the black crows flying over head and occasionally picking on dead bodies, while enjoying pieces of flesh throughout the rotten bodies of the enemy's army. They were happy that these undignified flying animals would not be able to pick on their organs. The Brave Man with the Queen of Peace, happy that they came out as victorious, departed towards the cave where they had kept hiding their kids and Ela. They were making wide steps and were in a hurry.

In the souls of the two existed the fear that they would not be alive, but this longing they did not express among themselves. They quickly passed the many kilometers and worried they pushed the rock of hope. Right after the gate was opened, the aggrandized eye pupils of the kids reflected happiness. Ela, right after she saw the Brave Man, jumped on his body. Was crying and saying:

-I thought that I would never see you again.

-You never say never, - he responded and closed her mouth by kissing her with the passion of entire world. The two forgot that they were surrounded by kids. Those kids that felt ashamed immediately turned their backs on them. Some others closed their eyes with their hands, and some others mocked at the girl with blue eyes that bowed her bottom lip. She wanted for this instant to last forever, but not in there being watched by others.

-Don't hate the people when they fall in love and are happy, - Melani said.

-Kids do not hate. We love, -responded the little girl. –Now they are replacing my parents, this is why we don't have enough time, or?

-Isn't this another reason that makes me drop my face, -said the little girl while leaving speechless both of them.

-War and love make us forget about time, my dear, - responded the Queen of Besa and looked upon the old lady that was surprised with the girl.

-We also want that this thing would end soonest, - she said and invited the kids to come out of the rock. Inside the rusty rock she left alone the two souls of love. They were close to one another as much as they were not listening at all. While keeping the kids from there, she said to them to calm down and to remain in a row with their faces looking upon the sea. She saw the pyramid beyond the frozen water, then the people gathered far away, but were not willing to depart. They were only roving around. Time was going by and the Brave Man was not active. Worry and wait became a burden ever more. Being late was not his ally. He did not know how to come out of that tornado. Not even Melani was feeling better. The old Lady, worried was looking at the powerless creatures that were standing in silence in front of saddened Nora and could not stay silent:

-We are only wondering and looks like everything is going towards the hidden objective of remaining here forever.

-Yes, this is the Field of Roving, - said the Holy Spirit.

-What does this mean? – said the old lady while squeezing her backpack tied on her shoulder.

-The fact that we stayed more than it was needed in the grounds of Evil and us going up and down are a testimony to the rebirth of Evil. If we continue to violate the restricted hours of camping in this field, Demon will become alive and we will turn into a stone. And in regards to Ela and the Brave Man, let them love each other because only love makes the hours go backwards and breaks the stringent measures. So take advantage of this and gather all the people, - said the dove. The Queen of Besa was breathing freely, and said to the Girl of Peace to prepare the people. And the loving couples now had come out of the rock and

were going towards her. The three had come together and pointing with their hands towards the infinite shore. They were convinced that the frozen part in front of them, would keep them, because it seemed very thick. Then they became all equal. They saw one another, and were couragiously touching the shoulders of the sea filled with icy covers. Kids were going after them, the warrior with his tall girl, Prince of Schwarzenberg, the journalist and the man that was throwing paintings time after time in the drape surrounded on four sides with old wood and at the end the army full of life. Flo and the sister had tucked their mom in the middle and were playing music. Brother and sister were playing until they made Nora to return her head towards the people and say:
-Thank you, Ela for giving me eyes to see the army of love, the most beautiful ever caravan in the world.

Chapter 20

From far away was visible the peak of the pyramid. In the chest of mysterious river had entered a heavy weight. The North and the quick steps of people were rumbling from one shore to the other. The thin flakes of snow that covered the blue space were not stopping the people from enjoying the beauty underneath the water. They were walking without thinking that a thick layer of ice underneath their feet would be broken. Suddenly Nora heard subtle vibrations that were coming from the frozen bottom. She saw the Brave Man in sorrow, because those vibrations started to move slowly the amorphous bed. Except those two, it was also felt by others. Everyone was overwhelmed by panic that the icy layer after a little would be cut into pieces and the deep river, very deep, would swallow them.

-The inner beauty will kidnap us soon, - the Midget Girl said to the Chieftain who was not leting Ela away from his hands. He was approving with his head and saw the lady cook that wanted to vomit. He saw the other people as they were moving and told them to go away.

Everyone run towards the shore except Ela who was pegged with the Brave Man and with four or five other boys, that were still sitting there. He kissed the girl in her front and said to the fighter to be careful. Neither she nor the other ones could move. They did not want to live her alone. Please run, run quickly! Every day we will have another victim. Leave before we all fall inside. Escape on all directions, but do not rest over this surface.

They were not moving. The knight saw them again and said:
-You are disagreeing with me? Leave right away, - I am telling you. Then under the whistles of cold weather, vibrations of ice and butterflies of snow that were hitting their face they left like a lightening towards the shore together with Ela who was confused by the loud voice and screaming tone of the Brave Man. Now there were only Nora and the Chieftain while running after everyone. The two were waiting for the volcano to explode from one instant to the next. Surprisingly, there cannot be seen any muddy waters below the ice. You could see only groups of big stones in many shapes and from the tiny cracks of the ice was seen a chrystal water with a human smell. With all dizziness that she had, the Queen of Besa was attracted by the shining and multiple stones that appeared similar to women bodies in the sea. Rocks hugged with one another were tucked together in the bed of the old river. The enigmatic stones were covered in a perfect way from the algae. The chrystal and those interesting rocks that delighted Nora at the beginning now were torturing her brain. The passion for great things and the beauty that was thinking that the Water World had magically created it, because the green roots were detached and the stones were not stones, but real

women. They were young and old women with hair even longer than their body. The eyes like a sea among the young girls that were standing over the ice made the Queen of Hell to understand that vibrations, that were extended had no relation with an earthquake. They were talking with her, requested her help and assistance to the Brave Man. But, when the women were reaching towards the solid surface while hitting with their fist the solid cover, something was stopping them. Someone was pulling them towards the bottom together with the disaster that had started to be heard over the surface of water. She saw the old ladies that were fighting with evils of sea. They were not worried about giving their lives so that the girls would be connected to free people, that were leaning towards the ice that was spreading apart. The thick ponytails were catching by surprise the men's necks full of veins and were holding them until loosing their breath.

Unfortunately some of the men were so powerful that while fighting with these ponytails were pulling them briskly and in a blink of an eye they were cutting their heads. But, this was less important to them because they knew that this was the last ocasion for revolution. There had come time for change. For freedom. For another life. Nora with her strengthened and powerful feet in the slipping cover was looking at her people that were still over ice, then below the river were the women and the Knight with his fiery eyes who was aiming and pulling out to melt one piece of ice where they were boxing. She wanted to help them all-heartedly, but she had something heavier that was stopping her, this is why she did not let the Brave Man to break the solid surface.

-No, don't do it! – she talked with her voice and body that were shaking! – they should liberate themselves. It's better for them to die today like people rather than tomorrow like animals, - she said crying, while in the eyeballs of the Chieftain was lightning and turning off the skirmishing fire. They both were watching the fight below the water and no-one was suspecting, that after a few minutes over its surface would come out a powerful fist. War was fading the greatness of that hand, which was ready to explode the cover of water full of magic. They both felt an insupportable pain, when barbarians were attacking their women and the hits of the poor ones were immediately scrambling the hair in the bodies of young girls, that were going with open eyes towards the obligatory end. They slowly said goodby to life and were hidding below the stone that was heavy from the legs of the old sea. The blueish beauty was folded together with the multicolored chorals. However, most women were hitting non-stop with the power of being free and from the sounds and loud screams the floor of slavery was tearing apart. The scream of the huge ice plaque was being felt. The powerful vibrations were loosing both of their balace and the voices of pain finally sat down the men and women on their knees. The eyes of blue girls were in front of the nose of Nora and the Braveman. And their welcoming was telling them "enough with one death." They saw how close they were and then how they disappeared and fell in water one by one. The crazyness came to an end. At the time when the Queen of Besa tucked one hand on her waist to pull out her sword, someone touched her hand. Was the first hand that came to freedom, was the girl of sea that did not only relieve her hand, but after herself was pulling even other girls.

-Welcome! – said Nora! – You see? Fate is not the source of uniting our hands, but war for a prettier future is. You may depart, then, towards the pyramid, - she said to her and herself went to the Brave Man who was lost after the pretty eyes, shining blue skins and from the fresh aroma of naked bodies of girls. Faced with great beauties he entered the world of man's lust. He forgot that someone loved him, that the cold water was refreshing his feet, that the ice was pouring the latest thunder. The scream of the solid cover that was partitioning, as it was saying "we are going fast, otherwise you all will slip in my frozen chest." Then Nora was shaking the Brave Man that was confused and while nervous said:

-Even you, are like all other men?! – And he responded to her:

-I did not do anything wrong, -only that the blue color betrayed me and with this color I was thinking to prepare a blue sky for hell.

-Ah yes! Now that the sea is scrambling you are thinking of painting the sky? –Walk please, run, and do not withhold your feet. Look at the hand of the sea how it is breaking. It will not hold us for long over its cracked back. The Brave Man was looking towards those areas where scary ponds were opening up from ice, was looking at the elongated hands that were coming out of the river surface, listened to the voices that were needing help and woke up.

Then with a sword he cut the strong surface of ice, pulled them, and, while escaping from the shore, was stepping upon the hands of barbarians. His powerful hand palms were breaking the fingers filled with the flesh of ladies, that were trying to leave in the last moment. After coming out of the water, women were harnessing life, but were not feeling a happiness. Personal Freedom was not their purpose, so they were pulling one – another with all the power and departed from the sea, which appeared to be expanding its shore making their escape even longer. As they were escaping quickly, they saw those men underneath their feet that once they touched the warm wind of life they were walled and fell inside the sea. Although they did not feel sorry for them, those women were crying and were pursuing Nora that already had touched the sand. The young lady went up to her throat and beaten up to her bone, did not understand why the blue ladies were crying. Their attitude was surprising her. They were free, but tears were covering their faces.

-Why? – she thought! She was looking at the fierce ice how it was softening up. Surprisingly their tears falling in the solid covers were dissolving and from the water were coming out innumerable girls that were going after the sisters with long hair. By then Nora understood that those were the tears of victory that were making a miracle. Those happy eyes were looking at the Brave Man, who was delighted by Ela in these moments, she was speaking and caressing his wet beard, while the Queen of Besa was surrounded everywere by naked shadows, that truly gave light to blinded hell, was looking at men that were confused from the color of skin of those girls with thick intertwined long hair, and whispered to himself: "The Chieftain was right when he said, that with the blueish of these ladies you can paint a beautiful sky."

Chapter 21

With a distorted face, the girl of the living world was coming around the man to draw his attention and to show to the Queen of Besa that even she was there. What was said "bla-bla" was about stopping both of them to talk about the triangle. While worried that everyone had forgotten about her, she was not stopping from talking with her gestures "that you brought me here to safeguard your world and liberate humanity, because I am in the middle of all of you to give a life to hell and to find the golden tower, because the two of us took your time when making love, and so and so...". This connection that was formulating the sentences one after another, would never end had it not been for Nora's interruption "that if the morning is not coming up in your world, we all will die, and so on...".

-No, no, we have not forgotten you, dear. You are our life. For this reason we don't involve you in the war, this is why it seems that you are on the side, but there is also a small thing that you are not remembering to say.

-What? – Ela was asking.

-Because you are not capable to kill.

This time she saw her awkward and in an ugly manner, it appeared that she wanted to swallow and if her mouth would not talk, her ass would.

-Ah, caressing according to you, is the inability to kill, - responded the lady cook.

-As I can see, you may be hurt from something else. Hey. Perhaps love?

-Exactly this is my power, - she said! – looks like, feelings are controling you, meaning that who loves and who does not kill is not a real person. For me, to be honest, is different, because I lived the sweetest and prettiest thing in my life.

-This is why you are dissapointed with me? Don't make my hell harsher than it is, please, - she talked and like a spoiled girl she entered in the wetted chest of the Brave Man. At that point Nora thought that Ela was clearly foolish. It had nothing to do with bitterness or jealousy. The opposite was true, she was not feeling well that after a short time the two beloved ones would suffer "for mistakes and their sins," that this caressing was brief and all her life she would be contemplating for that heart that she will never have close by. She was feeling sorrier that the girl did not know that she was going with the king of the other world. According to many projections it is impossible to have the seed of dead people in the stomach of living ones, but it happened and thought to herself while looking at the Chieftain that was holding the girl tight in his breast, but his mind was right where his eyes were directed.

Chapter 22

In the blue space the movements of people towards the castle were frozen again. Nora was worried and was looking around herself. She could not understand why all these people had fallen into this laziness. Everyone was busy with something and were standing in one place. The road was blocked by the painter who was passionately drawing those wetted bodies that were squeezed even more. In the painting, the first place was given to two shadows that were embraced closely, hiding behind a stone, that was only covering the bottom half of their bodies. Beyond them he was painting the blue ladies naked, that were taking a break over those skinny rocks, and in the background was predominating the black, while drawing the pyramid over the harsh rock edges. The Midget Girl was enjoying the drawing that he was making. She saw him how he was pouring the black color over the white canvas cloth, that was barely held by its wooden legs, but even this time the painter had closed the landscape within his sophisticated imagination, to continue his work latter or to leave it for now, because she needed him. She bowed a little and showed him the clock that she received from Ela, and the painter immediately stopped his work, because the longing of the girl was more important than his love for the arts. He went slowly towards the Chieftain that was grabbed by the hands of the lady cook and requested to him to bitter up his face acting as he was upset with the girl, because the way they sat together, the painter was not finishing this phenomenal drawing as he considered it. The Braveman understood his purpose, liberated his hands, kissed the warm girl, and climbed on his feet. Without keeping her away from his chest, they departed towards the triangle. Even the others took the same path without knowing what was waiting for them. The pyramid was growing ever more. They were discussing on who will enter and who would not. All of the people wanted to enter.

-Do you think everybody could enter? – the journalist said to Nora.

- Of course, everybody can enter, but we are departing for somewhere else therefore all of us cannot enter. To satisfy our curiosity myself, you, the painter, and Ela will enter.

-But why only four people? Take me with you, - said Melani.

-Don't you need my arrow? – was talking the Fighter with fanfare!

-I am not separating from you, my dear, - said Melina, the Girl of Peace and stayed close to the youngster's body.

-Can I come? – was heard the soft voice of the blue girl.

-Yes girl, you are free now. Come and stay together with us, meanwhile the rest of you can depart right away towards the Golden Tower. There we will meet again, - spoke the Midget Girl. The Chieftain with his brain into pieces in silence said to himself: "Here, perhaps begins the road of separation among both of us." He all-heartedly did not want to stop from loving Ela and did not want to leave her in the pyramid. He was afraid that the triangle would kidnap the girl faster than time.

"There is nothing else more ruthless, faster, but also slower than time," – was speaking his heart inside his chest. "It makes you a king then makes you a beggar." There is time for yourself, not for you. It deceives. It is happy because it changes its face every day. It does not wait. It does not care if you live well or not. How you take advantage of it, day or night? It feels sorry that it gives you plenty and takes so little, that she is tired with you. Is longing that people are killing for nothing, and always says: "go, kill yourself if you want, because you cannot kill me, indeed I am the killer." Always is proud that she is pretty, and you don't know how to enjoy. "Is proud for stealing the years and for gifting time and again stays with batters head down, because it cannot do whatever it wants." Yes, but she cannot do whatever she wants, - said the Brave Man and smiled inside himself. How unfair is towards, or? Hey love say something because I am going nuts. After the smiles from his inner chest were coming the shrieking of his soul that said: "Hey, do not worry. Love and the big ones kill time. Therefore, leave the girl, please. Leave her. She will overthrow him." Ela was asking, with whom and smiled? The man did not speak, he only releaved her body, opened his powerful arms and said:

-Pursue Nora and do not forget that we will meet at the Golden Tower.

-What do you have? I am not going there to die, - responded the girl with her pink lips. While she was kissing him in his silent front and left towards the Queen of Besa that was waiting her. The Girl on purpose had forgotten time and had closed her ears from the quiet waves of air that were whispering slowly: "hey, both of you cannot be together anymore."

Chapter 23

Through the great stones with emerald color were walking the long rows. They were going towards the Tower of Gold. The challenging roads were never ending, but however neither the number of people was ending. It appeared that from the dead stones were sprouting live people and were following the good soldiers. The blue women were adding even more light to the people with a full spirit, these women had just earned their freedom and invaded the space with a divine brightness. Their naked bodies were not allowing enough space for the imagination to men. They were ashamed for their nakedness, but they did not feel any mistake, because there were those men themselves, who never allowed them to live outside of the icy water. Those women did not know the meaning of clothes or a pair of shoes. However, they gifted the miracle to hell. Proud, silent, tied among their hands, they were delighted with the goods that were brought to them by the generous and good ones and went after the Brave Man with his broken shadow, that the air and snow were hardening his breath and his clothes were getting frozen. The separation was entering deeply, masterfully, ever more deeply in his body. This reality was squeezing his brain and heart. The wider shoulders under the red mantle were shrinking and his face was getting old. His beard and silver hair were not bright as before. His knees were losing his body balance and before hitting the ground, he looked upon the two headed eagle that was making a caressing voice over the shoulders of the Brave Man. The bird with two heads was saying to him: "don't be afraid from separation, because you are not separated from her. No, you have just started to be united with her. Half of your heart already controls her chest, my King."

The rapid moves of the bird in the sudden rain, then the blue women, the perfect lines of the shoulder and things that had come out of green rocks, were awakening the Brave Man slowly from the pond of "separation." He caressed the head of the eagle over his shrinking chest, straightened his body over the horse, and tightening the cordon, leashes of his horse, he turned his head for the last time towards the Pyramid and said: -None can control the triangle, with the exception of the almighty. And like a wind he joined the most suffering genre in the world of hell.

Chapter 24

The peak of hell was becoming a clear blue sky. The road to the pyramid, that was divided on the left of the eight people, who had decided to enter in the black triangle, was not so challenging. They were walking together. The Midget Girl, before taking the turn, was looking in the horizon towards the direction were the people of peace were headed. They were walking towards the home of Good Mother, and Ela was not understanding herself why she was separated from the Brave Man only to enter in that giant stone and to extinguish the curiosity of Nora. It appeared that she was disappointed because everything made her upset. Even herself. She had grabbed Melani by her arms that was ready to fall upon the sharp edged rocks and with her inflated nose was looking at the journalist, which pulled a pencil and paper from the beige colored bag and started to write something over the white paper, then looked at the painter, that, although he was constantly painting, he had not finished a single painting.

He was not stopping from painting the peak of the pyramid. The Lady Cook was even looking at the pretty girl naked who came close to the Queen of Besa and timidly asked her for the mantle of wool - Guna - that covers the shoulders. The girl wanted to cover her naked body before entering inside the misterious stone. Nora whose nick name was Midget Girl pulled away her mantle with broidery and shamed for not remembering to do this by herself, begged for pardon while placing her mantle over the girl's shoulders. The blue light girl extended her blue hands and instead of taking the cover she squeezed Nora and said to her: - You have to pardon me, - because I have always bothered you. From being nearby the Midget Girl was able to see a few signs of violence on her body. She was frightened. They were open wounds on the girl's flesh that were still pouring blood.

-Do they hurt? – Nora was asking while touching with fingers some deep lines over the fractured arm. She was squeezing a little, and then said:

-Oh, yes, they hurt more than never. These are the wounds of the world of isolation. In slavery cells are irreparable. The Midget Girl pulled her softly towards herself, layed her on her chest and said:

-There is nothing in the world that cannot be fixed? The cells of women are not irreparable. They feel pain, but they can heal. You understand? – was talking with her just like with a little girl that needed to hug her.

- Earlier you told me that you have become a burden to us, - Nora was talking again.

-Yes, we have become a burden for you, - responded the girl.

- In regards to this you don't have to worry because the burden of the dead is held by the living ones. You see that girl before us? – she pointed with her finger towards Ela that was walking before them.

- Yes I see, - responded the blue lady.

- The entire weight of darkness is held by her. The blue eyes full of light were pointed at Ela's body. Even though the lady cook was a little far away, it was enough for her to see the girl. From that distance was not a big deal for her. The shape of her body did not show whether she was developed or was a brave fighter. From behind was not giving any hints, that she was able to handle the whole burden of hell, but from the dress was not perceiving anything except the elegant mantle that she liked due to the color that was similar to the skin of her body.

-From the appearance she does not appear to be a fighter, - said the woman of sea.

- It does not mean that you have to appear as a fighter, but to be a fighter, that is what counts. Ela is a magic triangle. She is shaped by three powerful items, that very few people have:

good soul, healthy body and conscience. If a person has these three gifts, he becomes unbreakable.

"For the lady with a sky color, that Ela was a magic triangle, that she owns this and that were not clear enough. And if we start to explain to her it will certainly become burdensome for both ladies, especially for the lady that has just come into the shores," – Nora was thinking with herself and walked towards the single peaked heights. The girl whose tied hair was electrifying her neat body, was filled once with air, and said:

- I have just come out of ice. I am interested to know everything that has to do with freedom. What does it mean to be a free woman? Don't you think a free woman is like me now? Tell me, please! The Queen of Besa was surprised with what she heard. She thought that the girl was reading her mind.

-To be a free woman? Now you understood, - responded Nora! – you earned this name. Take a look at your fist how powerful it is.

As she was speaking, she grabbed the blue hands of the girl and continued to say to her while looking in her eyes:

-Do you see these skinny arms? These were the ones that won the trophy, meanwhile to enjoy the title that you gifted to yourself, do not hurry, do not get confused! Confusion often gives you unwanted direction. You are strong, you know how to wait for the right time. Therefore, you should walk slowly. This is important, - said the Midget Girl. The Blue Lady did not talk any more, she only grabbed the thin mantle around her body filled with wounds that were still pouring pain and quickly run through the sharp rocks with her wounded feet, that she barely handled. She bent down to see her feet. The wounds were deep. The weight of slavery was costing her in freedom because she did not know how to walk. They were used to walk in the clear water. This was the most beautiful think they had. While not willing to remember neither the good nor the bad thing of the sea, because the two of them were frightening her, she woke up and without looking at the stones with many shapes, that cut the bottom of her feet she was walking after the other ones. The pretty girl of the sea was surprised by the sweet laughs of the two young ones. She was looking up front and the eyes of sky fell above the bodies of those in love. The girl and boy were touched for not hidding from anyone. They were caressing one another and enjoyed when kissing each other's lips. They became surprised and it seemed interesting to them. They had not experienced nor lived such a moment before. She was not ashamed to see them openly. She extended her hands and with her skinny fingers touched her virgin lips. The man that was married, never kissed her in the lips. Her lips he was always touching with the back of his hand. Silent and wounded, the blue girl was not stopping from looking at the youngsters. She had started to see the prettiest parts of being free and her dark face was softened up, and the modern girl was not even worried that she was being seen by someone. She was happy with the young man, who forgot on being isolated, that with his arrow he had to defend even six other people. Opened to infinite caresses, he did not notice the war tools frictioned over the rocks neither evil running confused time after time after Ela while loughing. Like always, prone to ruin those plans, this time he had decided to be in the middle of hell's minority. The two exhausted ladies and occupied with the little evil, that was coming around, they were not seeing the stonned steps, that separated them only a few meters with the gate of black triangle. Melani was being abandoned and loosing energy. She could not stand above her feet anymore. She looked with her face towards the lady cook and slipped slowly without knowing where she was sitting. At that moment the Queen of Besa like crazy started to run towards the old lady and did not allow her to sit down.

-Don't, Please! Look below your body.

The old lady was stunted. Almost pegged to her foot was a human sceleton that was broken into pieces. She shivered even more when she saw before herself hundreds of stairs filled up with human sceletons, spread all over the place, that were moving with difficulty. She was sorry when looking at the bones trying to connect with one another. Everyone was trying to construct his sceleton just as it was before. As she was looking at the knees, the detached hand from the sceleton body touched the old lady behind her toe. She screamed and clashed with Ela. The screams of Melani woke up the Arch man who was succumbed into the chest of beautiful girl. Like mad he jumped over the skinny hand and wanted to turn it into pieces.

-Don't! – screamed the Queen of Besa! – Isn't it enough for you that your arm has not been detached from the other parts of your body? These bones were not happy in their "blessed" world, therefore they have thought of finding their happiness after death, and, killing the others, they would take God's place. Saddly they have not found a single pretty thing, with exception of flooded knees in the mud of pain, that are trying to unite them with their back turned into pieces.

Then Nora came close to the sword touched it and said the young boy:

-Here touch it, - take in your hands. Don't be afraid. You see? It is a sword similar to yours, just like mine. Caress it. It won't hurt you. The sceleton is only looking, through you to collect the pieces and to further enter in the pyramid. The Fighter took the bone hesitantly and departed towards the giant stone meanwhile the other skulls were rolling through the pavement of stone.

Everyone wanted the same thing just like their friend: to enter in the Kingdom of Father, even though they were suspecting now that he existed inside the triangle. Because they alone could not make this happen they begged the couragious hand to talk with their Creator. The knees and arms spread from the bombs were looking for explanation from the Father to explain that why, after death, they were in His Kingdom. They had given their lives for him. An explanation he owed to his own kids, that were cut into pieces. Ela shaken from the mouths that were talking went after the young boy and noticed how evil was crying.

-What about you evil, what do you have? – asked the lady cook! – you feel sorry?

-I am also incapable to handle this, - he responded and cleaned his nose with the banknote of paper that he had earned in a betting.

-There are so many terrible things, as even the bad ones would afford, - responded the girl of living world, to Nora that was listening, but that she was not convinced that Evil felt pain for people. Simply, she was not trusting his tears. She was more focused on the palms of her hand, as she was going on the stairs after the Warrior, that except the sword on his fist, was grabbing the arrow while looking the dark edges of the pyramid.

Chapter 25

The eight people were standing nearby the black wall. They were waiting for the gate of triangle to be open. Deafened and darkness was leaving almost everyone breathless. Even the bone was not moving anymore. Was standing quiet in the hand of the fighter that was not seeing anything. The Girl of Sea observed that the young boy needed a little light. Approached him slowly, opened her mantle and with the blueish of her body was brightening up the place nearby the people, who thought that over there was the door of the thick wall. The arrow fighter thanked the blue lady, then he returned towards the curly hair girl, gave his weapon to her and started to request her the entrance in the ruthless surface of the Pyramid. He was not finding anything.

Minutes were going by and there was no sign of any door over the wall brightened with a blue color.

-The Pyramid has an entrance, but it has no door, or, at least, I cannot find it, - he said, - and if we continue to search for a long time we will loose time. We should not have come here at all. I think it is better to go back, otherwise we will not arrive at the Tower of Love and will not meet with the Chieftain.

-No, we will not return, - said bluntly the Queen of Besa, - here there is something that will be interesting to all of us, we only must hurry a little.

-We don't have to hurry nor wait any longer. Let's go now to leave from here. The Chieftain needs our help, - introjected the Lady Cook who was eager to see them leave from that scary place.

The evil that was listening, was standing on the sideline. He had entered and exited many times from there and he knew very well what was hidding in there. When he was younger they expelled him for disorderly conduct. Since that day he was not welcomed anymore to enter over there and for this was thankful to himself. Now he was free to do anything he wanted. He was happy. Yes, yes he was happy, but on this moment he was missing his friends. He wanted to see them again and decided to show them how to open the door.

-Wait, - he said while entering.

-We will not wait any longer, - responded the Fighter whose sweat was running through his back.

- Why can't we wait a little bit more? – Nora talked with a sad voice. Ela was not talking. Evil enjoyed looking at them fight because they were being late. The Midget Girl was looking at Evil how he was entertaining. Then for his disappointment and the sake of Lady Cook she did not want to extend arguments any further.

- I respect the decision, - she said and headed to descend by those inclined stairs.

- Wait, - talked again Evil, - it is this simple to open the door.

Evil's finger was pointed towards Ela.

- You are the key of the Pyramid. It is enough for this girl to touch this transparent mantle that all of you think that it is a wall and all of us will get inside immediately.

- What are you looking at? – Evil asked her - remove the veil. Everyone was shocked. Even Evil was shocked. He was sorry. Was risking more than expected. He could enter but may not come out anymore. In the blue darkness the Lady Cook layed her two hands in "the strong mantle" and swore that she would bring the devil into a set up in response to him obliging her to open the doors of the triangle. For a moment the seven people lost their vision from a powerful light that came from the corridor of the pyramid, and Ela with her closed eyes continued to keep her hands in the air. She still had the impression that she was pushing something heavy. When feeling that she was not layed on any place, she opened her eye lids.

- Oh, this is magnificent, - she said! – we have entered in the World of Pretty Kingdom. Everything inside was like fairy tale. The marvellous light allowed her to see every detail. She was surprised. Impressed she headed straight to the giant columns, that were rising one after another with an equal distance between them. The bodies of stones appeared huge, at a point that the ceiling could not be seen. They were filled with unknown letters. She could not read the letters that were taped over the tall rocks. She had never understood this type of writing and looking at them superficially she went to the last tower. Over the body of the tall rock Ela saw a board filled with writing. They appeared ugly and abominable drawings to her.

"Perhaps who enters here must leave a writing", - she thought with herself!- "No, I will not endorse any writing without knowing what is inside. I don't want to do any stupidity to enter in history or to show that I have also been in the misterious triangle. I have no desire that my name remain in the list of those people with power that sign by mistake the fate of others." When she mentioned the most powerful she was shaking, and was looking towards the wooden pavement that was holding a heavy weight.

- Why are you stopping so often over the wooden floor? What are you studying? – the Queen of Besa was asking the Lady Cook. – I think that there are more beautiful things to meet than this ridge that is taking your mind. Ela did not say a word. She was analyzing the marvellous ridge and heavy stones on how they could not ruin the foundations. She believed that they had entered by mistake and this place was not for them. Saddened she saw the others. Everyone was busy around something. The Midget Girl, Fighter and the Girl of Peace were touching some of the weapons hanging through the walls that were hanging and standing below the paintings.

The tools of war, made in different styles of fighting, were very attractive for them. She looked at the painter that was drawing the pillars and then erasing them, because they were not coming up straight. And the journalist was writing over the white pages, and then squeezing and throwing them over the misterious floor. The blue lady, silent like the stone, was enjoying the marvels of lights without moving from her place. The last one was the Devil. He was deceiving that one day this space would be under his rule. His disorderly state of mind was mixing with humor. Was jumping from one column to the next, then hidding behind them and while pulling out his head, was laughing just like he was happy. He appeared to have the power of doing anything. He even hit his chest in showing his pride that he would be doing a journey without a problem around the Black Triangle. These beautiful things that others were enjoying through the space, were not interesting for Ela. She wanted to continue even further and then to exit quickly from that place. Tired from the requests of others, and, after refusing to write even a letter of her name over the board, she left the giant columns and turned to the Devil.

- Hey you, Devil! You said that you know this place, or? – the voice of the girl appeared to be suffocating that Devil. 'You believe that you know something about me'? – Devil was talking with extended syllables and was rotating his tongue through his irritated lips that were dropping fear. He made a turn and then made another turn behind the column of sin and then pulled out his head.

- Hey, - what do you have with me?

- You say that you know this place!

- Yes, and I know it very well. Is there a place that I don't know?

- Aha, very well! Sounds good! Don't you want to stay in my company? - he talked slowly and smiled sweetly. Ela acted that she liked his company and was walking adjacent to him while shaking her ass.

- Who me? – responded the disoriented evil and he approached Ela. He had a short body and reached up to Ela's waist. He straightened his body in trying to be taller. Was petting his bold head, touched his ugly tail amid his feet, was feeling his little horns over the rugged skin and thought of being a true male. "You are exactly for her body", - silently spoke his sinful though.

Happiness opened his dark eyes and right there he started to show his masculinity. He saw Ela's waist and slowly coming around her.

"Yes, so quickly he entered in my trap," – She was happy!

Who fell in the trap of whom, the Lady Cook understood right away. The Devil with demon like lust kissed her on the waist and then softly rested his head underneath the warm belly of the girl, whose head was burning. The warmth of Ela's body made the evil to think otherwise and the things that he was living on these moments were a miracle, and for the Lady Cook was the terrible sacrifice of hell. On how many seconds she would wait, she did not know. She moved her eyes as that would be her true love and squeezed her body like – not a single one but - a hundred thousand evils had bitten her at one single time. From nearby the Girl saw how those sins had made her sad.

Melani was following the situation. She knew that the girl was aware about the decision that she had taken, but contact with Devil had shaken her so much that she needed someone to enter in the middle, otherwise the plan was doomed to fail. Ela did not think that Devil would react so quickly neither thought of the Old Lady in responding so quickly.

-Hey Evil wait, - called the Old Lady, - you know how to love? If yes, Then not here in the pyramid and not in the presence of her mom. Do you know what this means for me? – was talking Melani with tactics without pulling her eyes from that ugly Evil. Bitter Evil, but without hope, that the lady would be his at one point, saw the Girl of living world and without knowing that she was fuming hate, he smiled to her. And then turned his face towards the Old Lady, and with his face yellow than wickedness, said to her:

-I am under your orders, you bad lady. You did suffocate me. So tell me what do you need from me, - said the Devil with a rough voice, that could not be understood well.

-First don't call me a bad lady. Secondly, I am not the one who overthrew you, but is life, innocence and love, - responded Melani with an ironic voice.

-From you I only ask to do me a favor, - responded Ela, and then I will pay this favor back to you. We want to know what is inside this Triangle. So help us enter and you will not loose anything. Evil thought of himself even more failed than before when God kicked him out of Paradise. Humiliated from "mom and daughter" he headed to the first column on their left. With his head down he made a few steps through the dark corridor that was distinguishing his miserable eyes. He came close to the door, placed his ugly hands over the iron bar, inserted powerfully his nails over the metal's surface, pushed it with the power of indolence, and while leaving his scars the Monster entered inside. The Voyagers of Peace saw one another, and without saying a word they went after him. Silence that was coming from the inner side of the gate made the three fighters to be careful before the fingers of their feet would step into the toes of Evil. They were a prey of unlimited curiosity and slowly entered in the unknown nest.

The Arch Fighter carefully revealed the white arrow arch in the hands of Old Lady that was shaking from fear and started to prepare the arch with the arrow. The Girl of Peace, Queen of Besa, Blue Girl, were overloaded with the weapons that they had taken from the wall, were standing behind Evil and pointing out to him, that they were ready for anything. This posture, almost manlike of those ladies gave a courage to the young boy to pass the gate's arch that was separating with Evil. And the others entered inside. The person before last was Melani, whose hand was caressed by a bone. The skeleton and the old lady were becoming friends. The last one was the painter who had fallen into a problem, because after many times of drawing the three powerful pillars and still they were not coming straight as he saw them. The painter was walking backwards and was jotting with a brush over the canvas until his nose touched upon a steel surface. The heavy door was closed without a noise and the seals, marks of evil remained behind their backs.

Chapter 26

The second corridor of curiosity was totally different. In addition to the cold temperature there was no light and darkness stopped the people once again. Although they were surrounded by insecurity no one was talking. Suddenly Ela remembered her matches box that was using in the kitchen to turn on the oven. That night she placed her matches coincidentally in her mantle's pocket. However, she started to be afraid, that it was only something that she would have wanted to have it with all her soul. But no! She had founded it where she had exactly placed it. Squeezed it happily and pulled it while caressing the stone. The match box was spiting sparkles, but no fire, and Evil delighted in seeing the girl unable to bring light back in that corridor, was having his eyes turn into green color. Darkness was Evil's favorite, endlessly, to do his ugly tricks, and the Lady Cook was not focused in him, because his task was over once the door behind them was closed. She was worried on how to turn on the match box in order to discover the mystery of Black Peak. When the Girl was bending over the columns of nervousness and her fingers were increasing the pressure over the steel wheel of the plastic filled with gas, a warm hand grabbed Ela's hand.

-Give it to me, - said the Fighter! The Girl did not listen. She was hitting the stone even more often while reducing the sparkles further and taking away her desire to see the unknown and to come out of there.

-Let me try it once, - was speaking again the Young man. Ela was disappointed and left her match box while annoyed, in the hands of the Young Man. He tucked the little tool on his fist and let it cool a little. Then he appeared to be begging it to turn on fire, he placed his finger over the "precious" stone and hit it slowly. A friction and the fire came just like magic. Everyone was happy. "But, would a meager light expand and run over the darkness of this gigantic place," – was thinking the Fighter and was holding tight the flame, defending it as it was shaking from the cold air. Frightened that the light could be extinguished after a minute or two, the seven people had increased their attention under the brightness that could not allow them to see no more than their feet. They were looking around maybe they would find anything that could contain the fire. The same thing was done by the Midget Girl who said:

-What is this here?

-Where is it? What can it be? – were asking all the people at once.

She did not respond. She was focused on the bodyguard, which was very close to her.

-It is similar to the angel, - she was whispering and grabbed the wool angle of the mantle while starting to delete slowly the dust. After she took the thick layer of the very fine sand with her fingertips, she started to softly touch the white marble.

-Oh, this is an angel! The body armor of the girl tucked behind the wall seemed very weak up to the bone. The towel with soil color was covering only half of her body. Her head lowered was kept in such a way that her clean tear was dropping straight on her hands made into a fist, that she placed over her naked legs. Her hanging neck and tumultuous face had gifted her the image of a woman, had become more succumbed into sorrow than an angel-like creature. The white hair had covered all her back part of the body and were touching the ground. As she was looking carefully the walled shoulders of hers, Nora felt sad and wanted to cry from that moment. Her two parts chest had no wings. She had them cut off. Oh God! Who made disgusting action, and why? The wings are cut but appears that those hands continue to be strong and powerful. Poor girl! – she was wounded in her soul knowing that she would never fly anymore. As she was looking every detail in her, was surprised when looking at closed eye lids that she moved slowly, very slowly and over her fists was dripping that tear. As she was looking at the eye lashes, the girl hanging on the wall opened her eyes that were bright like a diamond, and her lips spoke up:

-Do not have doubt on my disability. – said the Angel Girl with her wings cut. I have strong hands, that will be of your service. Let's go and let's light the flames on my hands, on the pond of my tears. The people were surprised with the bad luck girl. The painter, as always, started to paint, and the Queen of Besa, very carefully, extended her hands while touching the fists of the young boy that was holding the match and hurriedly releaved it on the hands filled with the juice of innocence, that was dripping through the wet fingers and falling on the dark floor. Immediately the tears turned into flames and the space was acquiring light right away.

Oh Jesus! What could you see: through the dead walls remained nailed hundreds of angels half naked. Underneath the white feet were carved a few writings, which the journalist could barely see. With much difficulty was uniting the little pieces of letters that were painted over while reading them with a loud voice "It is your mistake solely. All of you have no value. Now you may cry." Underneath the writing was included the text. "We take the courage. All of you no."

-Ah, - said the Midget Girl. – Someone who had tried and attempted, had cut their wings and had obliged them to drop tears in silence, in full darkness.

-Perhaps if they know how to share their desire, they could have passed the challenge, - said the journalist to her friends.

-It is easy to talk. You have the impression that we don't know anything? You are wrong. Whether you knew or not, had or did not have any luck, they would punish you one way or another, - was heard the voice that had come out of the white bodyguard attached over the thick wall with tears that were going like a river.

-Excuse me! You are right. I was stupid. Ashamed she crossed her hands over the chest that was still dropping red liquid. Particularly at that time she thought how often innocence could be killed. The Queen of Besa felt bad for the gesture of the journalist, but knowing that it was not done on purpose, she said: -Just like you she is also punished. Both of you are killed the same. From now on you are the light of hell. The angel, was sad and bitterly poured the fire from her hand in the hands of another lady without any wings while trying to spread the flames on every corner, and Ela with all her great pain she felt for them was searching even the space poorly lit. In the half dark space, she was waiting to see graves filled with corpses of pharaohs, that were relaxing forever in silence. But no. With the exception of long corridors and angel girls hanging over them could not be seen anything else. Her eyes were buoyed while looking at the ladies without arms. Through these walls she was looking for traces of torture, that were disappearing in front of their eyes. They immediately understood that the Lady Cook wanted more light so they were increasing the flames even more in the two sides of the Dead Wall. Their inflamed hands were beating the darkness. The light was controlling swiftly the tumultuous walls and was bringing out everything. The eight people were looking at the two sides of the infinite corridor.

-But what are these? Rooms? Photos? Hey, are these rooms? – they asked one another. Surprised and not sure on what they were looking at, they came close by to verify if it was what they were thinking about? These were not their eyes' allucinations. They were really rooms. Yes, yes, they were really photos and above every door there was a photography showing the face of a person.

-These types of things are over here? – said the girl and immediately she pinpointed her eyes inside the four angled frames in the unknown figure. Deeply focused in the letter that was maintained extremely well, she noticed that on neither one of the angles of the old frame there was not any decoration, official seal or a black ribbon that would normally show that the person in the photo would have been dead. Surprisingly, in the photo without a background was the face of someone, but without a name nor last name, without the date of birth nor death. The freshlooking photos were not works made with advanced techniques or another great work of famous artists. Simply, black and white, and were really close with the photos that always identify someone. She had seen hundreds of paintings and artistical photos that were elaborated or shot by the most famous painters and photographers of all times through different galleries at every corner of the world, but no one had attracted her so these pieces of paper that were hanging in the rusty nails from the sins of humanity, and undoubtedly were showing something extraordinary. The inner content of frames layed on the silent marble made Ela to forget what time was. For the second time forgot what she would never take off herself a minute and to gift it to her.

Chapter 27

Through the double darkness that was playing on every stone angle, the Hoy Spirit worriedly was hitting his wet wings in the middle of snowflakes. The mammal with a human soul, was sure that they were nearby the tower, but the monstrous darkness and bad weather had made the bird (mammal) to lose every contact with Mother of Love. Without stopping in the convoluted air with holy eyes, the dove was looking for the Rock of Happiness. In the dark space something was saying to him that over there something bad had happened.

-We are near and I don't like this silence, - he said to the Chieftain, that was suspecting that perhaps had lost the road and his broken mind was always standing on his half.

-Do you hear me? – was speaking the dove again! The man continued to lead the army acting as everything was in order. The Dove asked him the same question. He wanted to know, did he know that they were there?

-Yes, I heard you, but how to move forward? – responded the man with a red mantle.

-The two of us will go first to see the terrain, and the others let them wait here, - said the Holy Spirit.

-I want to come also, said the Prince of Schwarzenberg.

-No, - said the Chieftain. – You must stay with the people until I return. He revealed the chin leash on his hands and went after the spirit with wings, which was standing already over the peak of the Castle and was looking the palace from above, that was echoing death. The steel Knight had taken the rock. The confused bird was hoping that Mother of Peace was well and half of her people she had been able to save. With little hope she went below, and, standing two – three meters over the head of Brave man, she said:

-Dear King, they have occupied the Castle, but this stone has the Room of Prayer.

The man remained silent once and then asked how to get there?

-Give me some light, because I know were it is. Is towards the west and pegged in her walls. The room is big and the door is small and invisible to a simple eye. Cannot be opened without a code, but I know it. She entrusted the secret in me, - said these words and then stopped.

-The Castle had been covered by a black cloud, but the fire cannons over the wall, I believe that they would be enough, for us to go over there, because I do not want to use the fire of my eyes, they have a strong light and could awaken those bad people, - said the Brave man to the Eagle that was softly touching his hair with her beack, because the Eagle did not know what else to say.

This time darkness was at the service of the man and the Holy Spirit. Ruthless darkness was helping them to enter deeply and even more deeply without even being tracked by the enemy. The Chieftain was walking without any noise through the stones cracked from the occupation of the bad ones and was walking through the steel soldiers, who were fed up with the killing of innocent people, were sleeping quietly. He wanted to kill them all but had no guts. There were many, very carefully he was walking so that he may not step on those good people that were killed nor the 'living' dead in sleep. Turn after turn they arrived at the hidden place without any sign of life. The Brave Knight was opening and closing his exhausted eye lids that were loosing all brightness. He was not used to keeping his eyes closed in front of the enemies.

-We are at the place of prayer, said the Holy Spirit.

-Where is the gate? Was asking the Chieftain that had stopped and looking all around, then he raised his head in front of the tall rock dressed in a thin net that was heavy from dust.

-I cannot see any gate! We are wrong. Where are you going? All the way straight to the war? I am ready to either loose the brightness or to dissolve on fire and to give them a tour? – he said from inside that they would not be able to find the gate.

The Dove came nearby the thin mantle made over the whole surface of the turbulent rock, and said:

-The Gate I cannot open. You must do this, because here I cannot bless you anymore. Our work has been ruined since a long time ago. Please start. Here below the rock. Tear one piece of the net carefully, because if you ruin it totally, the echo will awaken the bad ones.

The Brave man was looking once at the Dove and then fell on his knees on top of the solid wooden patio and started to tear the mantle of a spider. He entered his left hand up to his elbow inside the stone and was looking amid the nest of the rock. Suddenly his hand touched on a steel object. He touched it slowly, grabbed it and pulled it towards himself. It was a round box of steel covered by glass and underneath the glass the surface was a white paper. The man was looking at that tool with great attention but could not understand anything.

-Read it! – said the Holy Spirit.

-What do I have to read? – responded the Brave man.

-It is a roadmap that anyone can read and if we do not read it appropriately, the castle will crumble.

-What is hidding behind this very thin paper that you are saying it must be read by each one? Say whatever you want, but I don't know how to work with this book.

-I will show you, - said the Dove. The Chieftain acted just as the Dove guided him. He pulled out the glass cover and the little suspension of aluminum had just come out of the glass, came from one side to the other. The Holy Spirit requested that with his closed eyes to remove the layer over the white paper. He closed his eyes, pulled out the thin layer and with his fingertips tracked around the second field. Appeared that he was touching into numbers, letters and a needle that was not moving. After the needle was not moving from itself made its hand in the shape of a compass and touched something that he was trying to mark on his head. After finishing up his finger sensing opened his eyes. He was surprised when he saw four letters melted in bronze. The letters: L-P-V-J,[4] - had turned their backs to one another and were not talking among themselves.

-Continue even further, - said the Holy Spirit! - take the pencil underneath the steel and with its sharp point pull every letter and place them together on point zero were the two segments meet each other. With a little struggle the Brave Man brought in the center the letter L. Then softening up he moved the letter P. With good manners he took the other two letters and finally all four letters were sandwiched by one another but were still moving to not stay together.

-Now, close quickly the glas so that letters may not escape. Hurriedly he turned the cover on its place, and, catching them off guard on the white field, closed the box of steel and placed it quickly in the square nest. After he pulled back two-three steps, the rock moved with the gate of stone that was moving slowly. From the halfopened gate there was coming a low light together with voices of exhausted people.

-the gate is opened, - spoke the Chieftain.

---

[4] L-P-V-J: initials in Albanian language that stand for; East – West – North – South.

The Dove did not respond. The man looked around himself and started to call the dove with a lower voice, but he was gone. Now he felt alone and weak before the mother's gate. His eyes like fire compared to the supernatural light coming from a woman washed in gold were nothing.

-Don't call him! He is gone to the Pyramid to get the others, - she said.

-There are no men in here? – she asked and moved her head to see inside.

-As I can see, the room of rescue is built only for women, or?

-No, because there are no men, but can you call those men who kill and enslave others in the name of manhood? – responded the Grandiose Mother and started to come close to the man who was bothered with his feet standing over the betraying earth of hell. On these moments, the Braveman felt ashamed from the name of man, but he also liked this word, because he was a man. He wanted to show her that all people were not the same. Wanted to hug the old lady and perhaps that woman would feel the warmth of man, who would die in saving those women. Since she was so direct, the Chieftain could not take the first step. His body was made so stiff, that if someone would touch him, even with a cane, he would be turned into pieces.

He did not like that she was judging him in the name of manhood. He was bothered that the Grandiose Mother had lost her faith in her sons, at a man that minutes ago united East with the West, North and South, opened the gate and was ready to die for them. He could not accept the fact that he had to pay for the other's deeds. Not at all. Distrusted and his acusations were irritating his hair. And, when the Brave man turned into her to say that it was not true, the Lady came close and said:

-I feel very sorry, my son, - but I had to difinitely test you. I cannot trust anyone. Please, excuse me! After the offensive words that had become a burden and then the word "excuse me" was breaking down the wall of sorrow and energy of pride of a man. He pulled her towards himself and mother and son hugged each other. The voice of heart inside a heart full of bravery, invited him to fall on her knees. He sat on the dry soil and with his head down he said:

-Goddess of Love! Please, do not let me go down without being born once more. The Lady full of brightness, covered with a gold mantle, ordered him to rise from the burned soil.

-I knew that one day there would come out a man who has not lost face over the deceiving goods of the world, and I, the mother and woman of charity, I swear in this night of pain "you will not fall until the whole love of the world is gone", because I am the mother and your servant, my son. Do not loose time while falling on my knees but go quickly and bring all those defenseless over here.

-It looks like slavery has not exhausted you, o woman? – the girl that was like a black boogy woman spoke. When she saw the man, she tried to fix the dark hair and her grey skirt attached after the body that had some sand in it.

-Love does not make you a slave, dear, but hate does, - responded the mother with a supernatural voice, and the Chieftain did not speak, but he did not like the lady with her face like a shattered leaf.

-Go my son and bring the people here, as long as the bad soldiers are not waked up.

The Brave Man waited until the mother closed the door and then he left. Once he arrived at his people, he asked them to separate into two: the fighters on one side and the elderly with kids on the other.

-What are you waiting for, all of you, old ones? Pass through the kids, - said the Chieftain.

-No! – an old man was against the idea, who was resting over the rotten rock. – We will not move from here. Don't dare to bother us. We are old, but you will need us. For us is not important how much we will live. How many times we need to say this, - he continued and then pointed his fingers to the kids. – Don't let these ones to die. The Brave Man did

127

not speak. He saw that it was impossible to change their mind. Moreover, through the disoriented darkness he took the kids and left them at the shelter of Mom, then quickly came to the soldiers, that waited for him in front of the black Castle. He saw the people how gigantic they were. They knew that the responsibility of changing the world of hell was much stronger than life, so this moment belonged to them. They had no words and were not looking for orders because each one knew his duty. Full of courage and the feeling of victory they were spreading around the occupied Castle.

Chapter 28

Everyone was busy with something, except evil who was occupying the middle of corridor. He had lived in that place; this is why he was not impressed with anything. He had never thought that he would enter there again, but what could he do to Ela that was pretty and wanted her ever more. With his disgusting thoughts he would not detach his eyes from her round waist and elegant walk, that she was doing in order to attract him even more. The girl, except her flirt with the Devil, was looking at those hanging photos over each one of those doors and was talking with the old lady to explain the meaning of that piece of letter framed with marble. The elderly lady was keeping in her hands the white skeleton that was breaking her soul in asking her to connect the skeleton's arm with the other parts of body. The old lady was caressing the bone but was also worried for Ela, because she could not help in explaining what those photos expressed.
-Come on let's go inside, - responded the Queen of Besa! – I think that someone is living in this room, - she talked without thinking on what was over there. Ela did not respond, but she took away the wing of her blue coat and saw the clock that was running the hours one after another.

This time she noticed the hour that was not accurate, but did not say anything, because every second she was convinced to know more on what was beyond those gates with photos. She walked a little then she stopped in front of the gate covered by dust. She observed once those people spread across the space of the corridor filled with light that were holding the angels and again turned her eyes into the photo. Her body was shaking. She knew it. Extended her hand to touch it, but she was afraid. She reminded herself that it is impossible to play with people whose responsibility for the fate of humanity lies on them even after their death. The face of man that had made the discovery of the century was not old at all even though humanity was suffering from his work. Mad from the fact that the man was recovering and was proud, she decided to enter. After she got herself together, placed the hand on the handle and entered inside. Under the double handed light, the girl of living world noticed the naked man. He was not like in the photo. Sitting next to the wall and with his head bowed was looking at Ela over the frame of reading glasses. With the two hands was trying to cover his intimate parts before the girl who no doubt would criticize him for his sins caused to humanity. He was weak before a soft lady. He wanted to say to the girl that what he had done he could never destroy, but his errors could be softened up by others. The man was silent because he was at fault. On these moments he desired to have two hands and to wipe his dirty face with his tears that were falling like a river and to grab, comb his hair that was like that of a zombie.

-Why are you crying? – she was asking! – why didn't you remember to do a better thing rather than destroying the world?

-I was succumbed by the desire to be famous, to be strong, - he responded. – Look beyond myself. There are plenty of people who are sorry for aspiring great works without thinking on what they are offering to the world. The light that was rising behind the shoulder of the Lady Cook, made it possible for her to see the other people that were suffering the punishment of hell. She peeked towards the left side of the naked man. She was scared. Some people with white hats were eating the arms and legs of a fat man's body. The man with his head half bold and with his low voice, was looking for sympathy from them by saying:

-I am already killed. – Yes, I am dead.

-What are these people doing? Why aren't they eating first his head? The man would be dying quickly, and these people would finish up their work right away, - said the girl whose stomach had rised to her throat.

-The head is going to be last. Those men want to inflict pain in him. They want him to suffer. They want the head to see what it had done to the poor body. Therefore, do you see how the successful banker has ended up? We have not deserved better; therefore our place is here. Turn your head on the right and you will see the happiness of good people. Ela was intermingled so bad that she did not know where was the left and wright. While she was searching through the room covered by marble, her eyes touched a transparent film that was vibrating like a colorless fruit jello. Although the layer did not appear to be thin, through that she was looking at things that marveled her. Thousands of people that were singing, dancing, writing, reading verses, smiling, and accompanying someone else who had come there.

In the wide field, adorned with multicolored flowers, through the wet grass were celebrating men and women. Each one was proud of their trophies held up in their hands. Like spoiled kids they compared the awards with one-another. Among the people, who were happy with their well deserved gifts, the eyes descended towards the man with a black suit and red scarf. Although he was fairly old Ela was attracted by his charismatic face, his small eyes, cute nose and sweet smile. He stayed with his legs crossed in the clean floor. Smart and quiet like anyone else, was talking quietly with the people that had surrounded him while looking at his scarf tied on his neck. The silk poured upon his body was covered full of medals that were shining. Everyone wanted to touch those things ranked on the mantle with a blood color.

-Oh! What if this man would have known that his people – whom he called 'my people' – now they hate him, are trying to change the name, to burn his scarf, to remove the photos from the wall, wouldn't you think he would feel sorry? – Was speaking Ela with the zombie man.

-The smart people would not feel sorry. They don't ever die, - was speaking the naked man. – do you see how do they live? I was also intelligent, but not smart. Look how I am right now. I would have better not existed. But why would I complain? I have not deserved a better place than here. I lost my soul and body in exchange of fame. And when I could make a choice, why wouldn't I chose the good option? Why would I be here and not be over there? How sorry I feel. Please, tell your world how great and sad the pyramid is, - was speaking and felt deceived from his works and his obstructed hands could not wipe out the tears of sin. Even Ela was crying. She felt sorry that the man had committed suicide with his right-hand.

-I know that you want to help us, - the man spoke again! – But, go. I beg you to go!

She did not move. With pain she saw his face covered by a black color and eyes that were vanishing slowly. The girl wanted to soften his pain. To tell him that...

-I told you to go. Go over there where you have come from and give a meaning to life exactly what every woman can do. Show to the people how powerful you are! She screamed so much that the stone started to shake. The Lady Cook understood that she should have come out of there right away. She saw again the divided wall amid the good ones and bad ones and closed the door swiftly. The seven people were gathered close to each other and were waiting before the gate to escape from the triangle.

-Have you seen the Evil? Where is he? – she asked Nora who had placed her hand before her mouth astounded on how bad they were suffering in the purgatory.

-Look, look! How good! You have not forgotten me? – he was smiling. – here I am, - responded the sadness, who was standing before her legs. Now he was convinced that the lady would keep her promise.

-Not only I have not forgotten you, but I will fulfill with delight the word given to you, - she was speaking while rotating her eyes that were radiating war, and the bad one even though he was very close to her was not feeling the smell of deception, of the intelligent lady.

- "After a while you will be a groom. The groom of the best creation and loved one by God", - he said to himself with pride. "What do you think the Divine is going to do now when understanding that the lady will betray her Creator?" He felt great, his saliva coming out and dancing from happiness that he was winning over the Holiness that once had thrown him from its empire.

- Naturally the poor guy is old and sleeping somewhere at the top, over there. Old age does not allow him to deal with his own creatures every time they call, - he was saying. While evil was dealing with God and his creatures, Ela was planning how to proceed and escape from fighting with the body of evil.

- "Let the Holy Spirit keep me away from this evil man," – she whispered under her nose.

-What did you say? – he was asking.

-No, No, nothing, - responded the girl. – I said that only time is going by, - and she almost said, her mouth almost slipped in saying: "forget that I will be yours, you the ugly one."

-Yes, you are right. We have nothing to wait any further.

The girl was electrified from head to toe, and he shook up, grabbed her hand and started to caress her soft fingers.

-Wait! – interrupted the Lady Cook. – Don't I have to remind you again that we will not make any love in front of my relatives? Listen, we both will salvage everyone from the Pyramid and in the moment we are alone, we will descend upon each – other. Ok?

They turned to the people, asked them to follow the Devil and take with themselves the angels with cutted wings. He did not like the idea, but this was the agreement. When he saw that there was no choice, he raised up his hands. The six people frightened were looking at what the lady was doing and what was her plan. Only Melani was sure that she had not lost her mind to satisfy the body and soul of evil. The lady of grey hair years was standing nearby the kitchen. She was able to keep the son of Demon away from the soft body of the girl.

Evil was leading them impatiently. Everyone was going after him through the multiple turns of the corridors. They treespassed the narrow and dangerous stairs while holding upon one another without looking at the dangerous abyss down below. They were walking in a row and if no-one would be slipping everyone else would be falling.

Women and men were breathing deeply as they were going up the spiraling ladder. The painter was overwhelmed by his worry to paint the stairs without any armor, but he could not even this time. Carefully he followed his fellow voyagers towards the triangle shaped peak.

-How much time do we have until the exit? – was asking the Archer the bad one.

-A little, - said the evil and when he was passing on the last stairs and reaching the plain surface of stone a powerful light brought him down. From that huge pain he could not open his eye lids. He fell with his face down and with his two hands he grabbed his head while screaming from the blindness. He was not capable to control anyone nor to move. He was almost totally paralized. Ela came immediately to him, she saw the sadness for a moment, then she went towards the door that was shining from the whiteness.

-Do you think there is an exit from here? – she said.

-No, - responded Melani, - look what is written at the door. Read "don't touch my gate but read the book of my guidance."

-Where is the book here? – was asking the Lady Cook! – I don't see anything.

-I am not understanding anything, - responded Melani with her voice that was shaking from fear.

-If this is the one, - said Ela. – This is the room of God. – Then why he doesn't come out to help us, - continued Ela? On those moments the Old Lady remembered the words of grandma, who had told her once "everytime I was calling the almighty he was not listening to me. He was sleeping."

-Is it true they are sleeping! – said the old lady to the girl. Under the anxiety of fear, she was not hearing, nor looking at anything else except the man of no religion that was grappling, and a small door over the top stairs, in front of which were gathered the people. The girl had to use ultimately the weakness of evil, otherwise she would remain there. She looked at the gate, then the evil, and run quickly towards the door. Without even placing the fingers at the door handle, the door opened-up. Was the Holy Spirit, that was telling them to go outside. The people together with the little angels managed to get outside. The person before the last was the painter, who was trying to paint the evil – the one expelled from paradise - while he was hitting the floor while rolling down.

- "This painter has exhausted us a lot," – was thinking Ela. As she was going away from him, Evil with all his power pushed his body to reach the lady cook. Unable to rise he was crawling like a snake and touched the lady from the mantle. She fell down, and he was going towards her shoulders. The girl was screaming from sadness because that evil was covering her body and the door was closing in front of her. From outside no one could help her. Was fighting with him but she could not escape. And when she started to lose her hopes that she would escape from his hands, a ray of power engulfed Ela's feet and hands and while hitting very hard she wounded the Evil really bad while hitting the ground.

-Hey, you see this? Your place is here, - screamed with all her voice and escaped, got out and closing the door swiftly said those words. Inside the black stone was echoing the scream of the man without religion (evil), just as a commet was exploding inside. The Lady Cook fell in the ground almost fainted. She was barely breathing, and the Holy Spirit was saying from above that the Tower of Peace had fallen in the hands of bad people and the Chieftain was needing them. In those instants Ela was asking herself "how is it possible that I brutally hit someone? Was I also fighting?" She felt exhausted, but happy, therefore she did not think much and requested him to take Nora, the Archer and Melina and depart right away. She would come later together with the little angels, after they find the Holy Book. With the head resting over the cold brick plaque, she returned towards the white girls and begged them to find the "Holy Book."

The ladies with their wings cut off started to look on every corner. They were looking everywhere, but could not see any book, not any testament. Sad they gathered and started to talk with one another, and see perhaps there were written letters that remained right where they left them, but no one had the courage to come in front of the Lady Cook and to say that what the girl was looking was non existent.

-What is new, did you find anything? – she asked them and extended her neck to see the ladies gathered in there. – Hey, - did you find anything or no? Please talk! Why have you stopped? You should look even further, away from here?

The little angels were quiet.

-Why are hanging, bowing your heads like this? How is it possible to happen like this? It should be somewhere, - she said and she rose slowly while holding herself adjacent to the old plaque so that she could not fall. She went around the rock of marble. Was looking at the square stone from her nerves she rose her fists. She wanted to bring him the stone, but at the very moment she felt sorry. She poured her hand palm over the surface of the stone and started to caress its dusty surface from disappointment. Suddenly her fingertips encountered something weird.

-Here is the "Holy Book", - said Ela, and her shrinking eyes almost came out from happiness. – Here is the book, - she screamed and it was truly the Writing of God. She tried to pull the book from the stone and to embrace in her chest, because she wanted to take it with herself to the world of the living souls and to see all its pages as she liked it best, but it was impossible. The covers of the book were tied together with the golden plaque and her attempts to pull it out were not working. Then she started to read the writings of God, right there. She thought that she was speaking with the voice of All Mighty God.

'When I created the first man, I did not call him a catholic or a muslim. I made him out of clay, gave him my breath together with the ten commandments. Although humanity has broken these rules latter on, I have never pulled away from my creatures, but, while you did not respect me, all of you have placed me into a deep sleep that is hard for me to wake up. Therefore you must go and spread the love that I have given to you, please! "Tell them that no one must commit bad things while using my name. Don't think in being myself. Do not challenge me because if I wake up, all of you will feel sorry."

-"Am I talking with the voice of God? No. It is not possible. Our knowledge is limited, in order to see and talk like the Holiness. He is mysterious", - was thinking Ela. She bowed, kissed the book and together with the little angels she departed towards the occupied Castle Tower, saying a farewell to the triangle of curiosity that was rewarding the people based on their merits.

Chapter 29

The caravan of little angels was turned into a light for hell. With the flames up and held up by the naked hands and feet, the wingless angels were walking through the cliffs of rocks that were drying their soul, but beyond the pain they felt a happiness when their wounded towers were sealing not only blood stains but also marking the traces of freedom. They continued non-stop to walk in the paths of the world that they had been looking for. Their free hearts were struggling as they were walking next to the lady cook and the old lady, who was barely holding the expanded bag that was pegged in her old body.

-Give me your bag because it has exhausted you more, - Ela said to her.

-No, - responded the old lady and jumped in a way that someone wanted to steal it from her. – For now I am holding it by myself even though it is for you and kept the load next to her old chest.

-For me? Who are you? – was asking the girl surprisingly. – What are you saying? It was not a coincidence that you were in the metro with me?

-The world of hell needed an honest lady like you, - responded the Old Lady.

-Who ordered you to bring me here?

-Those who lived once "The Winter of the Century."

- I don't want to speak for the winter that I left in my world, - she said under sorrow and felt a longing for the people, for the City of Vienna, for everything pretty. When she mentioned the bad weather going on over there, she had the desire to never return into the winter that her grandparents had gone through. Meanwhile, Ela cut into two continued to walk upwards through the cliffs of the forest while holding the old lady by her arm, who was falling in her knees from time to time from exhaustion.

Chapter 30

In the shining bed of good mother, the bad Chieftain was snoring like a wild animal. Even the soldiers were sleeping like dead over the length and widened cold space. No one was remembering over the nameless forest which was suffering from pain. Under the screams of fear the rock was speaking with the head rised like a tree branch, and with the bright eyes of the living stone was looking his wide body covered on every part with steel plates.

-"Quietness will not be very long, but you don't worry"- was saying. "They will pull your limbs apart, poor guy. But you, honey, why are you shivering? You have my body to defend you. Is tough my skin. I can afford to be stepped in and be violated by the soldiers of the bad army, until over me will be stepping the feet of good people, because the latter will expell once in for all the bad ones. Uf, my legs, I almost forgot about you. Hold on tight! Don't worry. Why are you numb? Be relaxed," – the Albanian forest was begging them to relax their body parts and rest down its cracked back, while keeping ears and eyes open. When the stone was relaxing in a drunk darkness, felt that over his bones were stepping the warm feet. A wave of happiness delighted his solid soul and happy was accompanying everyone in a row. Was looking at the white dove how it came from the earth and coming around in the sky showing to busy people the appropriate places, then he saw the Queen of Hell, Archer, the Girl of Peace and the Prince that were positioned first and were patiently waiting to destroy the bad people, who were still sleeping.

-Who are these girls? – the rock was asking the frightened stomach.

-I don't know, - the stomach was moving turbulently.

-Ok, you with a big stomach. But why are you worried? – he said and his eyes were following the girls of the sea. They were staying close to every fighter. They were covered completely head to toe with mantels of rain. They kept their heads down so that their blue eyes would not be noticed. They were smart to hide the water color of their eyes. For the eyeballs of a living stone those ladies were extraordinarily pretty. The stone was looking from below the mysterious women fighters and did not blame the stomach for being tumultuous and frightened.

- "Now you relax your limbs", - he said to himself and closed his eyes that he would open only after liberation.

Chapter 31

In the blind darkness the Braveman on top of the horse was saddly waiting. Was looking at the time going fast and Ela was not appearing anywhere, just as the Chieftain with a dinosaur face was not waking up. He had locked the door from inside and anyone attempting to break it or enter in the room by force, would be stoned. Since the person without a heart was sleeping there, his soldiers were without a soul, this is why they could not attack those people without a life. Earth filled with steel parts, was occupied by him, by those, by the dead.

-Thanks to the good, the bad one does not know this thing because he would definitely keep the Palace sleeping for the whole life and we cannot do anything, - said the Holy Spirit to the Brave Man.

-Then what should we do? – said the man.

-Leave it on me. I will wake him up, - said the Queen of Besa and went towards the small room where he was sleeping. Was walking next to the dead corpses. Opened eyes and mouths made her upset. She was walking very softly and carefully passing the steel armored bodies. When she arrived at the door, she started to knock in a way that made it appear as a code, that was known only by two people. She had to convince the Monster that the lady knocking the door was Ela and was searching for the Mother of Love to open the door to her. After she took a break from knocking, she started to call:

-Mother, mother! Please, open the door to me. I am the girl of living world. I want to come out of hell. I cannot find the road to return home. Someone is following me. Who wants to take my heart? I am exhausted from leaving!

-Please open it quickly because they will strangle me, she was talking and while placing her ears in the steel she knocked the door even stronger. After she stopped for a little, heard a voice that was coming from inside, which the midget girl was not understanding, but grasped that she had to leave right away. Then she left quickly towards the army of the Brave man, and without looking anymore, on who was she stepping on or not, was falling on the bodies of people who were rolling in the ground. The war errupted. The good ones attacked from all sides. Women and men were fighting againt the sleepy ones, meanwhile she was running like a thunder from the man with white beard who was not cutting his view towards her. Together with his sharp sword he was cutting everyone coming in front of him. His face was different and was fighting like crazy, but nonetheless the chances to save her were very few. When Nora was leaving the territory of the opposite side, she was hit right in the middle of her chest. The hit that came from the arrow turned her eyes into black. The lady fell down. The wool cover flew all of a sudden in the air and then covered her pierced body. She died right there. The man with a red mantle fell in sorrow, from the mouth of the Monster were coming nasty spits and happy mingling. He thought that he hit the lady of living world.

-I killed the life! – screamed! – I cut the veins of paradise, I cut her heart. Heart? Oh, how much I would have wanted to hold her heart in my hand. How much I would have wanted to feel its beats. They say that it is a muscle that speaks, that does tic-tac, tic-tac. I want to see how it would shrink from fear of me holding it and, after enjoying plays with it, I would insert it deep in my chest that piece of flesh that does not exist in me. Do you think that piece of her body would be staying in my body? – he asked himself full of doubts that that heart would not be escaping. He raised his hand at the level with his chest and before the face that was pouring hatered he gathered slowly the fingers at the shape of an oval plate and rotated his hand.

Saw inside the hand palm as he was truly holding something that he was not holding in the hand and did not know how it looked, he had only listened that, those who have this, known as heart, are happy. At that moment he felt weak. He was saddened for missing this, and he could never have it.

-Is not good that I am without a name, - he said. – However his sadness went fast and he talked again:

-I was without it and will stay without it. I am not worried. It is important that she does not belong to anyone now. The girl is dead and everything will depend on my hands now.While raising his left hand together with the arch that took the life of the lady fighter, he said with a smile! – Oh, my love, pardon me! Why did you leave? Why weren't you a little sweeter. I did not want to be bad with you. So, pardon me! – and he smiled in a pejorative way.

Chapter 32

Beyond the old giant stones was coming the burning smell of war. As higher the ladies were aiming to go the more were heard the screams of clashes. Eventhough they were in a hurry to reach the areas beyond the massive albanian forest, the little angels were under fear because they had never experienced war. They wanted to receive any recommendations from the lady cook. But what could she tell them? The girls had never carried a weapon in their hands. With all the pain those girls were determined to meet with them, although they did not want to abandon what they had started. As a result they would not stop. Full of sorrow they touched their confined arms and were thinking, what those men should do to them in order to make them look uglier than they were? A weak moment engulfed the girl with her stiff hair and she headed towards the lady cook.

-Oh Lady of the other world! – can you show me something?

-What, - responded Ela while caressing her exhausted shoulders.

-Do we also have to fight against those males?

Why not? – Ela said.

-Because my pain's weight over my shoulders does not allow me to fight. I was at fault and they all paid my rebellion. Remained quiet, and then, while touching her stringent arms, she talked again:

-What is going to happen if we fight with those men today?

-You could also die, - said Ela.

The little angel bowed her head and the flames through her fingers started to extinguish.

-Aren't we created to be punished and killed by anyone who wants to? – she talked again.

"Can the little angels be killed"- was thinking Ela with herself and said:

-No only you, but not a single woman was born to kill nor be killed, but to only give life and love. God has not created woman to fight and kill. But we are courageous, we can and have the right to do this in the name of love. Squeeze fear just like we are pressing these stones and do not fear to unite with those people that love peace. I know that if you kill you all will feel lost, but even if you don't kill you will not win anything. So you should select one: to loose or win?

The right to select gave power to those without wings, whose face was changing from one instant to the next. Quietly they were spreading the force of fire through one another and were not saddened anymore. They had a bounty of bravery to face those men, so they were going up the forest running. Were breathing with the shadows that reflected through the rock. The girls were staying now at the top of the stone. They had received already the wings of courage and felt stronger. They could see the palace just like it was on top of their hand, looking at the black smoke, that was going up just like a crown of clouds, and the flames of fire that were swallowing quickly the walls melted in gold. The girls were listening the screams of war and the suffering of people. The destruction was worrying them but made them stronger. When the feet of Ela touched the highest point of the rock she said:

-My dear ladies! I love you so much. Now you should leave and spread out in order to meet again soon. Her eyes were filled by tears. Feeling that many of them she would not meet alive again. Worried she went to Melani, and the little giant angels were looking the lady then the tower that was being abandoned. They all together with the voice echoing vengeance they screamed "Until today you, from now on is us" and begun to run like a volcano magma swiftly towards the war. The lower they went they could see less and less the highest point of the palace, but its walls were enlarged more and more. The two ladies of the sunny world without separating from one another were following the one without wings, but they could not walk with the running speed of those angels. After a while the old lady was tired and she could not continue walking in the paths. Attached by the body of Ela that was barely breathing, she requested to sit by a stone that could not cover their heads. They were squeezing in there and remained behind the rock. Suddenly the old lady started to move through the breast of Lady Cook. Shiverings had grabbed all her body and her dark lips were moving uncontrollably. It appeared that she was praying for the good ones or was punishing, cursing the bad ones.

-What do you have? – Ela was asking.

-"I am dying", - she wanted to say. – The "end has come to me", but no, she did not want to give her hints that she would be leaving her after a little while.

-Nothing, - she responded. Even though she was numb from the shivering of death, the old lady was still brave and kept alive by the breadth of wisdom. She was acting as nothing bad was happening. Was looking at the fight widdening and her eyes were looking for help and was waiting for the one that could not be seen anywhere. Waiting bothered both of them because one lady's head was cut, and to the other, were coming even close the screams of war. Now the stretched shadows of fighters were falling over the bodies of those women. They were shrinking their legs hiding them underneath the skeleton that was kept by Melani sometime over her head and sometime over Ela's head. That bone was proud that it was defending them.

Was jumping from one side to another and told them to not be afraid. In the confusion of war over dust that was rising higher and higher, a sword was cutting the air towards the body of lady cook. At that moment Melani cut the path of the sword with the arrow that turned into pieces in her hands. When the iron soldier turned towards the old lady to hit her, Ela pushed the fighter with all the power and the tip of the sword could touch only the part of the chest of the old lady and heavily wounding her. The fierceness of Ela brought down the fighting man, who became irritated and rose from the ground and attacked for the third time. When those ladies saw themselves impotent, the sword of the bad knight fell before their feet together with the gray face that made all of the ladies sad. Someone had hit her on the side of the neck. The silhouette of the man was bowing towards the girl that was keeping real close the old lady on her arms and was trying to keep her alive. Blood had covered the chest of the old Lady. The wounds were very deep. Her face was deeming from one moment to another. Before loosing her energy, she pulled the bag from her bloody neck, left it in the hands of the girl, brought up her blue eyes towards the chieftain and tried to say something, but her body was dissolved before moving her lips. The Braveman was looking at Ela that was holding the body of Melani still warm and her tears were like a river. She would have wanted to sit down and share the pain with her! But how much worth was this. What was the point of crying for the dead while risking the living people. It was a done job. The old lady had died. He kept her hand and she was shaking her elbows. Was not hearing what she was saying, and the Holy Spirit that was coming around the space saw that the man was in a big problem.

-Cry because the tears make you feel better, - said to her. She begged the chieftain by saying: - Pull it out, please, otherwise both of you will die.

He rapidly inserted his hands underneath the arm and brought her up. This time the lady Cook did not disagree with him. She bowed a little, extended her hand over the white face of Melani, closed her eyes, kissed her front and said:

-I loved your warm breast, my dear! Now you should let the soul to relax! She begun to cry at the arms of the Brave Man who was headed towards the west, towards the hidden room of the good mother.

-Stop! Where are you taking me? – was asking Ela the man with an eagle.

-At the Castle of Salvation, - he responded. – Please come because the time is going fast.

-No, you don't even try it, - he said while holding the bag even more so close around the neck. – I will stay here with you, with all the ladies. They will need me, for my support. If you want, you may depart, - Ela was speaking briefly.

-They need you my dear, but not now. You made them capable to handle themselves. You are not needed anymore. They have understood that it is not important if one part of their life is missing. They will replace it later. Now you need a safer shelter. The war is ending, victory is ours. Therefore gathered all together we will send you right were you have come from. There is your place for you lady, soul of light. She was covered by the charismatic body of the man that was running towards the room of the Mother of Peace, turned his head one more time and with his eyes filled with sorrow he said:

-I want to be with all of you, with you, until the time comes for me to leave from your world. I want to enjoy a second of freedom with you and then I will depart happily. I will share with my people how a small group of good ones were able to change hell. I will tell them that the bad ones can be overthrown with difficulty, but they can be overthrown. So please, don't tell me no! A little bit more and I will be far away. Oh, very far! I do not like to depart from this world as a wounded person. He was looking beyond the shoulders of Ela. Everything was burning. He saw that it was bothersome to defend her and his own body. To abandon the fight, he did not want. He could not leave along his people, the people of the land that he loved. Upset with the girl that was not listening to him, he squeezed her hand with disappointment and was running even faster, but this time towards the fight entering deeper and deeper.

Chapter 33

The Brave Man was fighting with one hand and with the other was holding tight Ela, until he reached the rock were the Painter and the Journalist were standing. After he helped her to jump on top of the big stone and was ensured that the soldiers of the enemy could not reach him, he returned in the war front, and the Lady Cook entered in the middle of the man and lady and from there was observing those people getting killed. Was looking at victory but also at the separation, and her heart was torn apart from pain. Saddened she rested her head on the shoulders of the Journalist and was looking at the white page of the painter. After she saw the lines of the pencil that covering the canvas surrounded with an old frame, she was overwhelmed by curiosity. The tip of the pencil was not stopping in creating the shadow of a fossil man that was flying in the air and in the right hand was holding a large sickle with a medium size wooden handle, hanging over the heads of the people. She thought that these bones were moving through the canvas filled with death and the sickle was aiming and pulling back from cutting the lives of those people.

- "This is death", - she said to herself and felt that her neck ligaments were detaching. Her body was dissolved in a second and her breath was almost ending. Ela was not doubting that the Painter was looking at death and was talking with it. She was looking at the wooden pencil that was moving up and down and the man talking to the skeleton:

-Hey, what are you thinking about that group of people with white hair? They appear to be smart. Aha, no, - he does not want them!

She quickly started to draw two other people.

-But what about these two men here? Look at their fighting skills? They are perfect! Look, the one holding the star with five points in his hat is very dangerous, or the other one with the star with six angles. Or, wait, look at the one who has covered his shame with a long beard. Ah, this is bad! No one is suitable to you? No? You don't want them? All right, - but you will remain alone. Hey, do you understand? Alooone.

-Come and get someone, what are you waiting for? – she kept talking and drawing.

He was trying to convince the mortuary to act in a bad way, to pull a marvellous drawing and then to become the most famous of hell and paradise. Bitter that he was ready to fail, was scratching his head and eating his nails. He could not stay in one place. He could not handle this situation. Saddened that he was not accomplishing anything he was frustrated.

-What are you doing? Who are you playing with my feelings? How come you don't need anyone? And while talking fast also felt sorry because was afraid of the sickle. Softened the sorrow and he asked slowly: -Tell me then, please! Who do you need? Walk, tell me. No one? What do you mean no one? Aha! You are saying that you don't need the people that don't understand one another, those people that kill women and kids and those turning paradise into hell for their own interests. You say, "since God and evil did not take them I don't want them either." You say, "let them be taken by whoever because earlier or latter they will be killed among themselves even if they escape alive."

-You are not understanding anything that even these people say, - was talking again the Painter! – if you are cutting the heads of the bad ones, you will do a favor to the good ones, - was trying to convince the mind of Mortuary to kill. – Sounds good, then take this girl with black hair, - was pointing towards Ela! – She is pretty. Hey, isn't it great to keep this pretty girl nearby every time you need? This time he was jocking. Ela took for a given the words of the painter and started to shake.

-What? But I did not speak with a loud voice for you to hear me, - the man smiled.

-You are asking me to say to this lady to not be afraid, because this is life and you are death. So, life cannot be matched with death, because both of you cannot stay together. It is impossible. So you will not take anyone. Today you are letting go whoever you want through your sword edge. Hey, are you surrendered? – the Painter was asking the pencil saddened that he was not able to finish the drawing as he was originally thinking. He was not liking a powerless death, who sat down in the rock infront of them. He relieved his weapon nearby his feet and waiting if the neck of anyone would be crossing coincidentally in the sharp sickle. The painter wanted to give the painting of hell as a gift to the girl of living world, and the sadness reflected in the old generation, she would hang the frame in the most visited galleries of the world, and the people to see that even mortality often would refrain from Evil. After the failure the painter was dreaming to be famous. He tore apart the canvas, threw it in the ground, stepping over it, and later it came close to the journalist that was often writing and erasing over the notebook filled with letters. Ela with the fear of a fossil man that was still there, saw both once again, then she placed her head over the other one's chest and not looking at anyone.

Chapter 34

In the western side were the Chieftain with a red mantle was fighting, liberation and light was invading the stone walls and the Knight with his face like a dinosaur still was not willing to surrender. He was giving flames to his fighters. The Brave Man with an eagle was looking at him from far away and in addition to the pain for his people, the man was sad even for the army of the enemy, that were killed only and only because their commander wanted the castle to be ruled by evil. After thinking a little, he stopped, saw the edges of the sword, the hands covered by blood, and said:

-"But what am I doing? Killing people! Is this right? Of course yes," – said to himself.

-"No it is not the same," – responded the brain. – 'To be free the man does anything."

-"However, I am killing," – responded the Chieftain. – Why don't we try to make peace, - He spoke to the brain that was in doubts in regards to ending the war. "Hey, let's try even though we are sure that we will need the magic of entire world to reach that stage, but perhaps it works out," – said the grey hair Chieftain to the organ that was brewing in silence, and after it was breathing air, he jumped over to the rock were the boy with a violin, squeezed in his chest, was standing. He saw him once and noted:

-Hey boy, - place the stick over the chords. Come on play!

In the face of Flo appeared the mimic movements just like a true instrumentist. He rose up to his feet, straightened his body, held tight the instrument on his thin neck, looked upon the leveled wood, saw the varnish that had not lost its brilliance at all, and after placing his chin over the smooth surface and moved his fingers over the board, creating sounds of freedom. The Brave Man under the pressure that was making to himself and the influence of good chords, his body was reflecting the sun. On top of the stone he screamed:

-Hey, you people, - do we want to make peace? Are you ready to stop the bloodshed? Didn't we fight enough? Say something. People from both sides were listening to the man with a white beard. The magic happened, the war stopped, and everyone was screaming in one voice:

"Yes, we want peace".

But for the Iron Man the word "peace" had the meaning "we surrendered."

-Ha, ha, ha, - he laughed. They are losing and now looking for peace, - he said to his trusted soldier at the left of his giant body. – You see, who keeps my side will not be sorry. We incur pain all the time.

-Certainly, - responded the man through his teeth that were cracking from fear of the unexpected if they did not accept the proposal of the other side. The Brave Man together with the brain thought that this agreement was difficult but wanted to give a last opportunity to those failed ones to get better. The eyes of the man that were pouring fire, were trying to calm down the brain, that was shrinking and waiting to receive the news, that will make happier or linger everyone.

-What do you expect, dear? – Said the Archer, to the Girl of Peace.

-Nothing is positive, - she responded coldly.

-Why?

-Because he does breathe the same air with us. The word "peace" he does not understand, my dear, - she said. Without even closing her sentence, the waves of the bad Chieftain's voice were shaking the whole bloody space.

-No, - he screamed again an extended "nooooooo" that everyone was surprised, with the exception of the Violinist that was not scared at all. He continued to play in the violin while twisting his body like a dancer.

-Didn't I say to you my dear, - that he is not a man? The boy of Arrow Arches came close to the lady with a curly hair, was sniffing the hair covered by an aroma of soil and

151

continued to farewell the Brave Man that was nervous. He thought that the man trying to be a good one, was speaking to someone, without anyone sitting nearby.

- "It was good to try", - spoke the mouth to the brain.

- "Yes, but we wasted time," – was responding the smart organ, - "These are the last hours for Ela. We have nothing to wait anymore. Either we lost or won she must be sent urgently in her world." Then the Brave man, filled with anxiety and disappointment returned by the Arch Master that was staying below the rock and said:

-You go to the girl. She is at the rock! Right over there. Do you see her? – was pointing with her hand towards the Lady Cook that was staying tucked in the breast of the journalist. – Take and send her in her world. We will fight until shaping and building the paradise of once upon a time. When talking to the girl, was listening to the shivering of the heart that succumbed her soul.

- But, I don't want to leave you alone, because you could get killed, - was responding the saddened boy.

-It is not important who will get killed from us. She must be saved, - he said. While looking at the red eyes of the Archer Man came down from the stone, touched the boy in his chest and whispered to his ear, "depart". He by himself grabbed the sword with the two hands and headed towards the direction of the voice, that was hinting death, and without noting the boy was not gone, but was following from behind. The Brave Man was not expending anyone. Was totally exhausted from the Evils of man with a face of a dinosaur. His disappointment had exceeded the borders of generosity. The fate of bad ones he left in the sharp metal that was also cutting the stone. He was not worried anymore from the screams of pain caused to the poor people, but he felt bad that over the shoulder of the weapon was dropping a juice with the smell of failure and without a surprise from the fact that they had no red blood like his, he was burning their soil under their feet.

The Archer through the turbulence of war was expediting the man, that, although older than him, left him behind. The boy had no more energy to follow the man, so he stopped to take a deep breath. He kept his hands over the knees and was looking the Chieftain how he was cutting the path towards the man of steel. Crumbled he heard that someone was coming nearby. Turned his head on the side. Oh God! What could he see. On his side were lined up thousands of ladies, that were waiting orders from him. Then the Arrowman returned his head on the right, then on the left and said:

-My loved ones! Are all of you ready?

-Yes, - the ladies responded and just like a lightening rod they spread on all sides of the rock that was violently under control. Thanks to the hatred they felt for the bad ones, the little girls had spent endless energy that helped them to be fearless. Except the flames that were shining the rocks and were burning without mercy everyone coming in front of them, they were holding the trophy of victory in their short arms. The blue girls had thrown the mantles that were covered and with naked bodies were blueing the sky. The ice breakers could not hold the feeling of shamed nakedness because they were men, that had taken their clothes as frequently as they pleased, while violently exposed on them. What was the meaning of one or two towels that were wrapped around the skin covered with signs of violence, to cover those parts identifying a woman, that men wanted with much desire like nothing else. They could even die for them.

Chapter 35

The union of ladies was helping the good people to liberate the space. The blue women fighters were grabbing the weapons from the steel fighters. Those men were asking for their pardon, while saying "forgive the evil because everything will be accommodated", but their prayers the ladies were cutting with swords and every request for mercy was dissolved by a sword. In these moments the Archer had remained without any conscience. Tolerance was not anymore present in the inner world of ladies. Was looking at the bad ones that had started to renounce. Some were gone rapidly, and the other part were joining the good soldiers. The latter made her even happier because they were becoming more and more. As he was looking those women how they were fighting, he remembered that he had forgotten to return Ela were she had come from and had even noticed the Brave Man that had entered deep in the territory still occupied by the bad ones.

-Oh, God! Where is he? And she, where is she? Oh God, help me!

Although God was old and sleeping, the boy was searching in vein around himself. His eye pupils were widened that you could only see his white part in the eyes. From sadness, the sweat was pouring through his disorderly hair that was coming on his face or at times in his wet neck. The concerns of the boy were bothering the girl that was fighting half spirited with the steel soldier. After killing him, the Archer Fighter came nearby and asked:

-Why are you confused?

-Where are they? Help me to find them!

-To find whom? – asked the girl.

-Oh God, - where did he go? Where is she? – said and was running without knowing whether he was going in the right direction. The Girl of Peace with her curly hair understood why the boy had been succumbed in this condition. The bad feelings had overwhelmed him from head to toe. She did not follow the boy anymore. She immediately headed to the rock where the Brave Man had thrown Ela with his hands. Now the Black Hair Girl was stepping over the steel skeletons that were covering the Earth. This thing did not stop her even when she was hitting with her feet the sculls turning into pieces. She wanted to find the girl because someone needed her close in his last moments of life.

Chapter 36

In the middle of the smoke of fire the Brave Man was remaining in front of the face that was like a wild animal rather than a man. The two men, on top of the horses were looking at each – other on their eyes. The Chieftain with a red mantle that was waved by the wind, was surprised, how ugly was his enemy. He had never imagined how terrible he was. However he was not frightened at all. He saw him deeply in the eyes full of hatred and started to talk without coming close to him:
-Who are you? How did you come in this life? I don't even know, I don't care, but I know why you are here. In regards to myself, I was born from love. I was happy until the bad one...
-The bad lady, - responded the famous Knight. The Brave Man did not understand what was he saying through his teeth filled with saliva, so he continued to talk:
-As the Evil closed us inside the rock and interfered in the lives of people that wanted peace more than paradise, today I offered peace and you did not accept. It looks that it was not enough what you had done so far. How I would have wanted to be friends together, but you cannot afford this!

Therefore I want to stop my brain, oh creature of hatred! The bad one heard carefully the words that went to his ears like an offense. Convinced that he would be killing him with great ease just as he "locked" Ela, he pulled swiftly his sword from his belt and pointed it towards the speaker by saying to him:

-Please listen to my story, - oh son of Evil. My father had me with the beautiful evil lady who grabbed his attention. It was tragic, because he could not take more than this from her. I hated my father so much and killed him with these hands. Here look, with these two hands, because he gifted his body to my mom and not the brain nor that piece of flesh that you have in the left limb. The man did not allow her more than one happiness, while letting himself inside the beauty that convinced his brain. The poor lady, accepted and was connected to him with the hope that one day she could steal from him those parts that God, after a while gave us, again took them away from our betrayal. But the poor lady did not reach this stage at all. Then myself, the son of a man and Evil Lady, remained without wisdom nor a heart. So these thing that I know, you don't know, you stupid man! Listen, I belong to the family of Man and Evil. And what is even more bitter for you, your father is also my father. He loved you infinitely, while he did not feel the same for me. He gave everything to you through his love with your mother. This sad story was told by my mother who did everything for me to be where I am right now. And I will have them today. I will be the owner of hell. You know why? Because you cannot kill me, because you are born from love, or? For this I hate you and all those people, that were born from love between humans. Today I will kill you, just as I killed him. Yes, yes, with these two hands, I swear!

The Brave Man was shaking before this confession. His brother was not throwing at him some sort of joke and was ruining his brain cells, because to have a brother like that was a destruction. With his eyes closed, inside his body he was looking for the truth.

- "No. This guy has nothing in common with me. He is lying. It is impossible to have as a brother this sadness."

He opened his eyes and was looking. The mouth patterns of the Chieftain of bad army that was roving around in space made him remember the words of the father when he said to him "be careful, from your relative, even more than the unknown men." The man with a white beard did not accept that in their veins could be flowing the same blood. He was shaking once, gathered his mind quiet well and said:

-I don't trust you at all. Go and lie to someone else. As a brother I may have anyone, but not you! – He was totally ruined and hit his horse on the back and departed straight "towards his blood" while screaming with a loud voice that all space was shaking. The soldiers of both sides were standing surprised. They were listening to the Brave man stating:

-You are not God and cannot be. You are only a person, and a bad person. So don't think that I am afraid of you. Tell your mother, that with all the respect I have for mothers, how much my mother would cry, you should cry for the miseries that you gave to your son. Then the swords were hit so hard that it appeared like a loud lightening. The fight was fierce. The two chieftains were well equipped with armor.They showed a versatility of movements, they showed the greatest hatred they had for one another. The Chieftain of Bad Army gave a heavy blow to the Brave Man that the latter fell from his horse, while making him remember that he was his brother. And "the brother" at this time was thinking, that right there would be the end of the man with a red mantle that covered his face. For the son of Eagle this act was an awakening. He said to the double headed bird to leave from his chest. Grabbed his fists strongly in soil and right away rose to his feet. He rapidly touched the leash of the animal like a rhinoceros and brought down the two monsters in the

157

ground. Now they were equal. They were fighting with their feet in the ground. The Brave Man was defensive from the sword of his contrary who cut his red cover-mantle a few times. He was defending himself but was also attacking constantly. The man with grey hair, even though he was successful to hit the enemy a few times in his body, was not able to wound him at all. He had pierced his left chest completely and still nothing was happening. The bad man was not falling nor blood was pouring. He could not kill him. He was worried because was becoming tired and did not know where his enemy's weakness was to be found. His body was covered by the sweats of failure. He felt that after a little while he would be finished. He was not worried about himself, but about his girl and others.

-Where is Ela? – he thought! – who will retrieve her in her world? He wanted to stop here and enjoy hell with her. No, I will never let him!- he screamed, and, right when he wanted to hit in his right, the Bad Man placed up front his shield of steel and due to the powerful crash of a steel with steel, the Brave man's sword slipped from his hand and flew, was locked in the rocks. The Man was looking at the sword and then to the eagle, which departed flying to enter between the two men.

-Don't! – said the owner! Don't become prey to the evil hunter. You must not die. You will join Ela in the path to her world. The bird stopped. Was looking with pain the Brave Man who was exhausted and had no sword nor hope. Felt sorry to live more than her lord. But her guiding lord ordered the bird to act this way, and the eagle should have acted accordingly. Saddened like never before, was attempting to rise with his arms above the dust that was drying the tears of his sharp eyes. The Knight when he saw the bird going away, run towards the locked sword. The bad knight was happy to hear that Ela was still alive. He was saying to the Good Knight that was walking on his hands and knees to take his sword inside the stones, from this moment on the girl would be his. The Bad night had opened his arms and was hitting chest with pride, because he was the most powerful of all. The Holy Spirit was observing that war among the two leaders was not going that well. They were "brothers" and it could not enter in the middle. The Brave Man for any reason was not killing the bad man, so he left towards the Mother of Peace and knocked over the door of salvation. She opened the stoned door and fading was talking to the Bird:

-Hey, the Brave Man was in danger, or?! You do not need to tell this to me, - Otherwise you would not have bothered me. Is he alive?

-Yes, - responded the Dove. – Come on let's go together.

-I also want to come with you, - was saying the little girl with her white hair. I want to hug her very much and to say, that I have loved her as much as Ela. So please take me with you, please!

Chapter 37

Hey old man! Old man! Are you looking for the sword or what? You are struggling for nothing. It is hidden way deep. This way it does not appear that you are looking for the sword, but you are trying to hide, - was saying the Bad man while smiling with an irony. – Hey are you ready to hold it? Walk faster and take the weapon. You may hit me anytime because no one will kill me.

Then he twisted his rusty cheek and by betrayal he knocked the back of the Brave Man, who was still looking for the sword that he abandoned a while ago. He did not make any screams of pain. The wounded body was hanging over the rocks and was dripping blood.

-I killed you! Didn't I tell you that I am capable and much stronger than you "brother".

The Chieftain did not move at all, and the Steel Man fell in the trap of thinking that he had killed him, but he was wrong. He was not fed up with it. He wanted to cut his head and to pull his body through the sharp rocks. Until he would come close, the man with a turbulent hair had just pulled up his sword. After he had squeezed it was waiting for the enemy to come even close, and at the moment, when the Son of Lady Evil wanted to grab him from his hair and to cut his head off, the Brave Man screamed:

-God is not a twin. Quickly he hit with the steel edge penetrating his stomach and encountering the arrow of the Archer, who let down the arch and headed to help the hero whose blood was pouring. As the young fighter was pulling away from the feet of the bad guy, that had fallen over the body of the Brave Man, he was surprised. The breath of the bad chieftain layed in the ground was not going away, but a warm wave covered his body. The red blood of the man with an eagle was giving him strength that he even started to move his lips, and the good Brave Man was shaking. He was overwhelmed by shivering that he had not known before.

-What is happening with him? – was asking the Archer his own Knight.

-I don't know! Come nearby and listen what is he saying, - said the Chieftain.

The Boy fell into his knees immediately and placed his ear at the mouth of a man with steel clothes.

-Oh, I have taken life so very late! It is beautiful! – he said to the Archer, and his tears were falling on his warm cheek.

The Good soldier was showing to everyone what was saying.

-It would have been marvellous had he understood this earlier, - they were saying. He must have had the force in the blind gut. He must have thought and lived all his life in blindness.

-A sin! – was saying the wounded man and saw his skin that was turned into a charcoil.

The two mothers at that moment were nearby their sons. It was hard for both of them.

The mother of Brave Man was sitting next to him and was squeezing him in her chest. Was not crying. Was caressing his front that was slowly turning cold. The other one fell on her knees and crying for her son. She saw him dying. She understood how the kingdom, that she had dreamed with her son was crumbling forever, that is why it was impossible to stay without doing anything bad for the last time. Hiding she pulled the knife from the belt of her son and wanted to hit the Mother of Love in her heart. The Man of Steel understood the purpose of his mom and suddenly, with the last energy he grabbed the knife from her, and with the other hand hit her with a sword in the head while saying to her:

-You are at fault for teaching me only hatred. Mom and Son lost their lives at that very same instant, meanwhile the Brave Man at that moment felt pain, languished for his half brother.

Chapter 38

The clear crystal memory of the Brave Man gave the energy to his body to crawl slowly and to rise on his feet. Already with the image of undefeated man was standing before the people, that were waiting passionately their Chieftain to say a few words. While happy that he was standing in the air, he saw the bright space that looked gorgeous from shining light. His soul was relieved and joyful when looking at the grounds filled with people that had defeated evil doers. But, in the middle of thousands of eyes the Brave Man was missing those two eyes, meanwhile the deep wounds were warning him that after a while he would fall. His pains were exhausted and wanted to take a break. He was not so much worried about his wounds. He was talking to life. He requested to life to stay a little bit more. Yes, yes, to stay even a little bit more in the inner circles of his soul.

-Death and time we can never stop, but pain can be postponed even for a little, - was saying the Brave Man to life and to the wounds that were dripping blood. – They are giving us a hard time for nothing because I will not stop from looking even one more time at my prettiest woman.

Old and young men were looking at him with attention how he was cooperating at those moments with the last particles of life, that were barely holding his exhausted body. He was strong and almost nothing was happening to him, he asked the little girl with white hair, who had tears falling on her face in hopes that she could find Ela.

-Don't you see her? – she responded?

-No! Why, where is she?

-Here, next to you.

At that moment the extended arm of Ela stopped the pressures of pain. She warmed the freezing shoulders that were dripping blood. He touched her hand and while earning strength from the love of that woman, was looking at the Old

Lady, Archer, Eagle and the Holy Spirit, that were standing close to him.

-What do you have? Hey? Why are you looking at me? I am wounded, but alive. You think that I will fall. No way, the Oak tree cannot fall with only one hit so leave me alone, - he said to those around himself and left. Even though his knees were shaking and loosing the equilibrium, he headed as he wanted to participate in the dance of eagles. He rose at the top of his finger tips, was looking at everyone and while struggling to squeeze the hand of Ela, he still continued to talk:

-For hell and evil I was only a candle that was burned today from those that don't want light. So, the burned candle is not radiating fire anymore. However, I am very happy that we were successful to overthrow that evil. Today is extinguishing a candle but are scintillating and shining millions of chandeliers! – Then he took a deep breath, turned his head towards Ela, and said:

-Hey Girl from the other world thank you for the love and life that you gave to the people.

At that moment she squeezed his hand and wanted to hug him, but he continued to speak with the people.

-Don't feel sad if I am not staying with you, because I am here. Now that hell is gone someone has to stay nearby the Mother of Peace and to stand in my place. In my circle there are no squares. I equally love you all, do you understand me, but I will give my ring to the Archer. For me all of you are much worth than this piece of gold. So you should get along with each-other.

While respecting it and each other, you will love me and yourselves, all of you should not be attracted to the river of disputes, hate and dirty wishes. If you are committing these errors and entering in these waters, your happiness will disappear. All of you should embrace the infinite source: Love! Stay away from hatred you good people! Please!

Ela was looking at his face darknening quickly. His end was nearing. She did not want this end, but "without an end there is no beginning" was thinking with herself. The girl did not know that she could give a life only three times. These three possibilities she had expended, and she was waiting for the arrival of this difficult moment, and then to resuscitate him forever. Was looking at his hands, once powerful but now were shaking as he was pulling the ring from his finger, then after he brought it up to a point that his hand could reach and break the air and showing it to the people that were crying, and touched the Archer's hand, that was standing at his right side, and said:

-I swear and promise all of you that this ring will not be anything more for anyone carrying it, it will only be a sign that will remind you that I want all of you always united! Without even placing the ring in the Archer's finger, he was shaking, because the terrible pain was ruining his wounds and the time was engulfing his soul, and his heart wanted to return at its own place. His knees were exhausted, but surprisingly he was not falling down. He was kept energetic from the voices of his people, who were committed and determined that Peace and Love would reign even if paradise and hell would come around. Even though the Brave Man in these moments wanted to hold forever the hand of Ela, felt that his fingers were becoming senseless little by little, until he fell down. The crowd of people was crying from pain and then remained silent. The Archer that was nearby, was quickly trying to offer help, but the Brave Man refused. His eyes were pegged at the Mother of Peace, who sat quickly and cleaned the blood around the mouth of the Brave Man. The Brave Man sitting on her lap was talking quietly:

-I am very happy to be sitting nearby with you. No, wait, there is another greater thing that makes me even more happy. Freedom dear mom, and even if I had six hundred years I would melt them only for you, only for my people, oh

Great Lady. But, pardon my dear that I am leaving you alone. I am passing away.

-No my son, - you are not dying. Today you are at dawn in order to be reborn tomorrow. The Sun does not fade away, the son of my soil. This is the gift that good men award to themselves, - she responded and started to caress his weakened chest. His blood was dripping, and his veins were drained quickly.

His body, was freezing cold, could not move at all. Was looking at Ela with a crunched sadness looking upon him and sometimes looking at the watch at her left wrist.

-Time is going fast. You must return were you had come from. I am sorry that I could not do anything for you, my dear, but come close by and give me a kiss, and take what is yours, - the Brave Man was talking with his lips in a slow motion.

-What is mine? What do I have to take from you?

-The Heart, life, because I cannot give you the entire love. I will keep a little love for myself, - he responded.

-I did not give you all these so that you return them back to me. These three things have no conditions,- and kissed her with the energy of his soul, so that in the very same instant the Brave Man grabbed some power and raised his left hand and while caressing her neck so that she would not go away, collected the fingers of his right hand in the shape of a cup, placed in his chest that was torn, pulled his heart quickly, that was turning into a blue color and with the same speed placed his heart in the chest of the Lady Cook. Everyone was surprised. The man was holding the girl against her desire. He gave her the heart while leaving his body at peace. From his toes all the way to his neck he was stoned, but life was doing the last fight. He kept the eyes open and all fire of his body was relinquished to Ela in her frozen eyeballs. She was accepting fire unconsciously, and the blue heart had just entered in its own craddle and was becoming red with the living blood. The two halves were very happy to be united

165

together. At the time when the two parts were connected well, Ela fell powerfully in the ground. Opened her eyes and took a deep breath. The Lady Cook came back into her conscience only when everything was over. She headed again towards the cold body of man, while kissing his cold lips. Was licking her lips and caressing his blood veins. She could not stop fighting to bring him back in life. She was butchering her chest to bring out her heart and to insert it again in his opened wound but was not working. Was screaming, calling upon her warm tears falling from her eyes, in order to warm up his face, feet, hands and soul.

-Oh, no, tears cannot warm up the soul, - she said and started to call God. But God was sleeping. When she understood that every effort was worthless, she stopped and kissed the traces of his recent wounds. In those moments pain was flowing like a volcano and silence covered the surroundings. The little angels stopped their flames and the blue girls covered their naked bodies with the mantle of heavy darkness that succumbed all rocks. The Mother of Peace was not comfortable looking at the saddened Ela. She did not like sorrow. Through the darkness she saw the eyes of Flo with a violin that he had put down, saw the eyes of little angels and the eyes of blue girls and said:

-You, oh brother, - why did you stop playing! You should start a new song now! You little angels should light up the lights, and you girls bring more blue spirits to hell.

-So today we have a party, - she continued and turned her head towards the girl. – What do you have? Why are you upset? The Brave Man took from you three things. And one thing he returned back to you, one he kept for himself and the third one he gifted to you. The Lady Cook was not understanding, then she saw her with a surprised look.

-What are you looking like that? – said the lady. – You in your world could not live alone with a one half of heart, love was separated in half and one third..., - she whispered, and then kept quiet.

-What is the third? – asked Ela surprised and meanwhile she felt a soft pain that was coming from the bottom of her stomach.

-Now I want music responded the old lady. – I want light! Hey what are you waiting for? Hey you people enjoy life! And you, lady, be blessed.

We will miss him a lot. You must go now because time is threatening you.

Ela had no choice but to leave. She saw the peacelovers, who encouraged her to leave. She saw the eyes and tears squeezed of the little girl that remained pressured after the blue mantle and felt sorry to detach her skinny body from the mantle. But she had to do it. Then she came up front while saying to her:

-You are very capable to understand that I cannot stay here any further. Therefore saddness does not reward me my dear lady with a brash hair.

-Thank you for letting me understand that I am not an orphan anymore, - she responded and was squeezed strongly in the chest of the girl. While kissing her in the warm cheeks, she continued:

-I will love you forever and will be missing your presence, but you may go peacefully because there are other people who will take good care of me. And again, I love you so much, - she said to her and then jumped and swiftly entered in the golden mantle worn by the Mother of Love that she had close by. Ela was not decided, she wanted to stay but also wanted to leave, but there was no such option. She had to leave. She saw the watch and the eagles roving above while searching the gate of the sun. She noticed that she had a little time to greet them, but what could she say. She was thinking for a minute, and said:

-My dear people! My arrival in your world was not important for some, but for me it was very important. At the beginning with the Holy Spirit you gave me the first signs that I was entering in a misterious world, I did not know

167

what was happening. It was frightening. Indeed it was very frightening. Especially for a simple Lady Cook who does not know anything else besides cooking, she is not even an expert cook. When I entered in the Earth's crust of yours, I was surprised. Everywhere I could not see more than three types of people. Sleepy skulls isolated that were walking, but were walking backwards. The first ones I did not try to wake up because they liked to sleep. The latter group brought me sorrow, this is why I chose all of you here. At first site you did not appear friendly. All of you were cold people and not united. After a while both of us changed. Within a few hours all of you were multiplied that much, so that now I cannot count all of you. What was the source for us to be united and be so powerful?

-You, - responded all of them in one voice.

-It is not me; it is all of you, - she pointed towards the crowd. – you are the ones that embraced life. The crowd was screaming. She was counting the seconds of the watch and continued to talk:

-All of you are millions of happy people, but the happiness of my heart you may not have. When I leave from here I don't want all of you to be sad, because I am not leaving you, but I am taking each one of you with me. Meanwhile she grabbed the small hand of the girl that loved her and said:

-I will miss your pretty eyebrow, the most beloved one of under earth.

The girl with silver hair was not looking at her as she was talking. She was afraid that her tears would betray her. With her head down she responded:

-I also love you.

Ela was caressing her hair and while in a hurry opened her brown backpack and started to dig inside. She was looking for that thing that, according to Melani, would save and rescue her.

-What? How?

She was surprised.

- In what is this leash going to help me while walking over these polished rocks? With such a short chord I will be able to go up? And after she pulled it out of her bag, she was struggling to find one of the chord's extremes.

At those moments the eagle came in front of her face, grabbed in her beak the leash, hit her wings and flew towards the open space. The more she was pulling the chord was becoming thicker and longer. Then after the bird passed the gate of earth, tied the chord into a stone plaque and emmited a voice from above, inviting the Lady Cook that she could hang on the leash. The Lady Cook, surrounded by those happy people, tried the leash, then she was looking at the man with a black horse and promissed to him, that when meeting again in the world of the living, she would not be afraid anymore. With a smiling face he greeted the girl, who was holding tight the bag in her chest, she closed her eyes and headed right back towards the direction where she came from. A lightening appeared over the castle of marvels. The free souls, living hearts and the call of mothers to bring love, were turning again the burned tower into a golden spot, and, under the sounds played by brother and sister, under the blessing of Holy Spirit that was spreading powerfully in the horizon, while cracking all of the obstacles, Ela was passing from the dead world into the living world. She turned her head for the last time towards the Castle and said:

-I will burn for your voice, the saviour of my people! Wait for me, my love, I will return for my other half that is tucked in you, - and continuously was steping the stones at night towards the sky. She was leaving behind the under-earth, was leaving hell and paradise, peaceloving, evil doers, poor and rich, betrayals, and loyalists, dictators, democrats, thieves and honest people, singers, longing farmers, philosophers, religious believers and atheists, deaf people and those with big ears, pesimists, optimist, blacks and whites, yellow and red people, intelligent and stupid, attractive and ugly, but they all were equally the same.

The End
Vienna, July 2018

Translated from Albanian Language: Peter Marko Tase (Milwaukee, Wisconsin; May 23rd, 2020)

Short Biography

Angjelina Marku was born on July 16th, 1968 in Gjakova, Republic of Kosova. Mrs. Marku obtained a teacher's certification diploma from the "Bajram Curri" Higher Pedagogical Institute in her hometown and for a few years was active as a teacher. She writes prose and poetry. Has participated in many poetry and literary events, received a number of awards from various poetry festivals. Mrs. Angjelina Marku is a member of the ''Aleksandër Moisiu'' Albanian League of Writers and Artists in Austria and is a member of the Executive Board of revista ''Dielli Demokristian'' ("Democristian Sun" magazine) in Vienna, where she also lives with her family.

"Winter of the Century" is her first novel.

Advanced praise for the "Winter of the Century"

Book review

An enormously powerful story where the Albanian History is perfectly integrated into the world of literature. The Balkan's literature finally has an author in Angjelina Marku whose fiction style is a fulcrum for future generations of writers. With Ela and Melani, Marku raises in the summit of attention the role of Albanian women in the history of this nation and sacrifices made for its territorial defense. Meanwhline Nora and the Braveman reflect the perseverance, gallantry, and loyalty to Albania's leader, reflected as a chieftain in this volume. With the opening of Melani's story all the way to the battlefield we have in Angjelina Marku's book some of the greatest moments in European Fiction, uniquely depicted characters in world literature and the reader will appreciate the permanent clash between the underworld of evil with the sublime world of freedom fighters, defending their people and homeland.

European Literature has rarely seen a similar style cultivated in Angjelina Marku's writing; this is a piece of art that will resist the winds of time and constant evolution of style.

This is indeed, an intellectual treat: beautiful writing is not incompatible with geographical imagination and historical flair!

The early intellectual training and life stories in Kosovo, have prepared Marku for a life of humility before white men – or male writers that are always in fierce competition among themselves – but through her characters in the "Winter of the Century" an enormous influence has acquired the history of Albania and through the "Brave man" and "Archer" we have indeed preconceived aspirations of the author to install (unline any other previous writer) the battlefield of freedom in the first trench of theme then move on into other sub topics that for Marku's prolific work is fundamental and set's her apart from other writers.

This theme, which has implications far beyond the obvious go and evil parallel, is skillfully handled. The clashes with a sword among knights and world-renowned fighters are wholly absorbing. The nightmare experiences of Melani with her husband and the always attractive behaviour of the Lady Cook, are some of the memorable moments of Marku's lightening of success. The understanding of evil's role and the rocky landscape makes all climax a naturally driven scene that embraces the reader unlike any other prose.

Angjelina Marku's novel is absolutely an intellectual indulgence: attractive writing that is not incompatible with her nation's historical flair!

MARTIN BARILLAS, Former U. S. Diplomat, Journalist, and writer
Flint, Michigan
May 10th, 2020

Review of the Novel: "Winter of the Century"
Silence of the truth
Angjelina Marku is a movie editor having in mind scenes in this novel which goes one after another as within the movie. Of silence. But, how to explain that silence within the novel because the storyteller should be loud within her expression to move our inner soul towards understandings of her goal? It is very simple.

Namely, the biggest pain is mute. Silenced. That is why she is loudly muting within the world of current civilization showing us the forgotten world from the edge of civilization who were not guilty ones for anything, but only being human. Simple as it is.

Being in the same time within the capitol of the one of the oldest kingdoms of this part of the Europe, Vienna in Austria, she looks like a butterfly in the modern jungle, the insect with a wish to find a final place to rest before vanish into the dust of hope.

Her hallucinations are an alternative reality, which empower her to survive within the area of many, for the purpose of one. Within the time when she is the only sad person on the ground. Multiple personalities presented within this novel are just a reflection of the lost soul of the writer who, having them written on the paper, becoming fulfilled person, above all.

Cold winter and snow as a synonym of closeness and rejection while people interactions are melting all the boundaries of their thoughts and restrictions. Through the devotion, love, and care. Extinction and darkness vs. interaction and light. Within the soul. Of human. Being faced with the death in vivo of her close relatives and even a soul mate.

Death is a part of living and living is a part of death. All depends on the way how we look at that. She, Angjelina, decided for the second one – "living is a part of death" and we can see that through the entire book. Re-read the book. To understand the meaning of death within the life. Of hers. Although, we all came from the Energy and we all will be back to the Energy of love.

God? Yes, if there is any real one. For her there is. Above all, as the silence of the truth.

Assoc. Prof. Dr. & Dr. Honoris Causa Sabahudin Hadžialić
Sarajevo, Bosnia and Herzegovina
5.05.2020

Book review for "Winter of the Century", a Novel

As an avid reader, passionate about Kosova's Literature "Winter of the Century" has enriched my understanding on many conceptual themes embodied in Albanian literature. What attracts international attention towards "Winter of the Century"? Today, many writers use almost the same monotonous style of writing that limits speech and understanding rather than enhancing literature with all its facets and constantly evolving rhythm.

Angjelina Marku has done just the contrary; she has embarked in a journey of passion towards exploring the new paradigms of literature and its closely knit connections with a reality of war that is deeply ingrained within the nation of Albanians in South East Europe.

The Kosovar author has provided the reader with a series of personas, a legendary chieftain and women's role in historically critical times; all of these fully fleshed out elements are spine-tinglingly exhilarating and make the reader become engaged on those versatile scenarios that make us travel through time, that is almost as if myself traveled to these battlefields in the Balkans.

This book is like a dystopian drama that is richly developed within the framework of Albanian culture and realities of war, let alone a fully developed language that is really close to future trends of literature and avoids allheartedly a style called Newspeak, Marku has adopted a rather lucid language full of rigor, passion, indulgence, romanticism and patriotism. With Melani as one of the highlights of this novel, Angjelina Marku emerges as a genuine European author, that connects cultures, geographies and preserves a suitable coexistence between her nation's history and Europe's vital cultural assets.

Richard A. Brosio, Ph. D.
Professor Emeritus
Ball State University

PUBLISHED IN THE UNITED STATES OF AMERICA
MAY – 2020

ISBN: 978-1-71689-767-2
Imprint: Lulu.com

www.ingramcontent.com/pod-product-compliance
Lightning Source LLC
Chambersburg PA
CBHW060646260626
47161CB00008B/3021